Daughters
of
Magpie
Cove

BOOKS BY KENNEDY KERR

Daughters of Magpie Cove

of

Kennedy Kerr

bookouture

Published by Bookouture in 2021

An imprint of Storyfire Ltd.
Carmelite House
50 Victoria Embankment
London EC4Y 0DZ

www.bookouture.com

ISBN: 978-1-80019-965-1
eBook ISBN: 978-1-80019-964-4

For Caroline and Jennie, my sisters

PROLOGUE

There were shadows everywhere in Magpie Cove.

Small Cornish coastal villages like these were full of winding streets and tiny alleys the sun couldn't penetrate. It might glint through a crack from time to time, but only for a brief interlude on its journey from rising to setting over the sea.

The light was good in Magpie Cove: it drew artists to the village more and more these days, more than Connie remembered from her childhood. Then, Magpie Cove had been virtually deserted apart from the families that lived there and the fishermen, like her dad and her uncle, that set out to sea in the early hours before the dawn and watched the sun paint its living flame over the water.

Yet, the brighter the light, the sharper the shadow, and, one summer, Connie had found some in Magpie Cove. Streets and corners where she felt she was being watched. Even her own house, where a shadowy presence pushed cruel notes under the front door for her to read.

She never knew who it was who watched her, or who left the notes. Her mum told her that it was just someone who was jealous of her, that it was nothing to be frightened of. But Connie was frightened of the person that followed her home, of the pebbles thrown at her window at night when everyone was asleep, and the shadowy figure standing under the street light outside.

It was all such a long time ago now that everyone but Connie seemed to have forgotten the strange little notes that had appeared here and there for a couple of months. But Connie hadn't forgotten that summer, and it made her memories of Magpie Cove just a little less bright than they should have been.

1

'Needs a lick o'paint 'ere and there, maid, but I'm sure you'll do a grand job.' Connie Christie's uncle Bill stood by her side as she looked around at the interior of Magpie Cove's Shipwreck and Smuggling Museum. Cobwebs hung from the high rafters and dust clouded a bank of glass display cases, which, Connie thought, searching her memory, possibly contained a variety of stuffed sea birds and maybe the crumbling warrant for the arrest of a once infamous Cornish pirate. A draught was blowing at Connie's ankles, and there was a distinct smell of mice. It had been many years since she'd been inside the museum: the last time she was probably twelve.

'It's... lovely,' she replied, remembering her mum's admonitions to be kind to her uncle who was, in her mum's words, *offerin' you a proper job at last, so don't look ungrateful*. 'I'll do my best to take care of it, Uncle Bill.'

Connie had had a *proper job* for some time, in fact, although her mum had never seen it that way. She'd trained in theatre at university, despite her mum's frequent suggestions she *should have tried business or cookin' or somethin' else useful*, and then worked her way up to stage manager at a theatre in Plymouth, far enough away from Magpie Cove not to have to visit very regularly, but close enough that she could stay in touch. Unfortunately, the theatre had just closed due to a lack of funding, and despite calling up all the industry connections she could think of and scouring *The Stage*, she hadn't found anything.

'Well, you might think about changin' some things, I'll be bound. Young blood an' all that,' her uncle wheezed as he led her up the rickety wooden stairs to a mezzanine level. 'Now, 'ere's where we keeps most o' the photographs, though there's these swords, an' these chests too.' He walked slowly along the narrow walkway that lined the two sides and the back wall of the museum, pointing at framed pictures and display cases as he went. ''Ere's a lovely set o' oil paintin's. Smugglers' ships be like these, in the eighteenth century.' He coughed, holding on to the wooden banister for support. 'An' on this side, we got artefacts from a couple o' wrecks. The *Amsterdam* of 1749 and the *Lady Anne*, that was 1690, mind you. Straightforward shipwreck, not pirates that time.'

'Mmm,' Connie replied without much enthusiasm. If her mum, Esther, wasn't such a pro at making her feel guilty, would she ever have agreed to come back to Magpie Cove? Even having lost her job, she'd resisted, but then her money had totally run out, she couldn't pay the rent on her flat anymore and it was Magpie Cove or sleeping on friends' sofas, homeless. Even then, Connie had held back: there were things here she didn't want to remember. Yet Esther was relentless, seeing an opportunity to have her only daughter back home. *Your uncle can 'ardly stand, my love, we needs someone to take over the museum. An' I'm not as good as I was, neither*, she'd said on the phone, adding a cough for theatrical effect. Connie snorted at the memory: her mother was as strong as a cart horse. Still, Esther had been right about Uncle Bill.

He turned to her, his white beard catching the light streaming through one of the grimy skylight windows on the roof. He was her mum's oldest brother, sixty-three to her mum's early-fifties and Connie could see a huge difference between them. Bill had always had a beard, and nowadays it was more Santa-like than ever, resting on his chest and curling around his ears. Yet, last time

Connie had been home, Bill had looked his usual hale and hearty self with a broad chest and arms roped with muscle from years of taking the boat out, fighting with the Cornish tides. Yet now, her uncle looked thin. Connie wondered when he'd last ventured out on the *Pirate Queen*, an ex-fishing boat he'd turned into a tourist attraction.

'What is it, Uncle Bill? Mum was a bit vague.' Connie held out an arm for her uncle and he took it gratefully. 'I mean, you're past retirement age anyway, aren't you? You could have got someone in a while ago to take over.' She steered Bill carefully back along the mezzanine and they started slowly down the steps.

''Tis my heart, the doctor says. Plus the rheumatics don't 'elp,' Bill wheezed. 'Wants me ter stop smokin' a pipe as well. I smoked since I was in the Navy – don't see why I have ter stop now, not done me any 'arm.'

Connie raised an eyebrow but said nothing: stubbornness ran in her family. You might as well tell Bill Christie to stop breathing as leave his pipe behind.

'Anyway, keeps me busy. I didn't want ter retire. What was I goin' ter do, sit about the 'ouse? At least 'ere, if people comes in, I can be useful. Tell 'em about the 'istory of the place.'

The smell of her uncle's pipe smoke was intertwined in Connie's memory of childhood in Magpie Cove: along with her mum's Sunday roast, playing on the beach with her brothers as the sun set and her dad calling them in, yelling that it was late, it was getting dark. Since she'd arrived back in the village the day before, she'd been assaulted by the sounds and smells of her childhood like she was every time she visited, but this time it was different. This time, she couldn't treat it as a brief trip down memory lane, or use it as an amusing anecdote to tell her friends in Plymouth. *Can you believe my mum still fries everything in lard, her arteries must be like fire hoses. You know there's still only one pub in the village, right? And it doesn't even serve food.*

This time, she was here to stay. Connie felt the weight of what it meant to live in Magpie Cove settling on her shoulders like a dusty woollen coat. If she lived here, it was different to being *from* here, which could be laughed away or even used as something amusing at dinner parties: she was the girl from the tiny coastal village whose uncle was a real-life fisherman, whose family had lived in the village since the Doomsday Book, who hadn't been on a plane until she was twenty-five and hadn't eaten anything spicier than a Cornish pasty until she was eighteen. She'd used her mother's surname – Christie – since she was a teenager, rather than her father's surname. Her dad's name had been Berry: not unpleasant, but she preferred the way the two Cs sounded.

It was those things that she talked about to entertain her friends, even the ones that had also grown up in Cornwall, but more cosmopolitan places like Truro or St Ives, or over the bridge in Devon. They liked to hear her tales of remote, rural Magpie Cove twenty years ago as much as anyone. Yet there were some things about growing up in Magpie Cove that Connie never talked about – the shadows that lurked around certain corners, the streets that she never walked down. Things only she seemed to remember, but that she desperately wanted to forget.

This was her life for the foreseeable future – until she could get another theatre job, and that was looking pretty unlikely in the current climate where arts venues were finding it harder and harder to stay afloat. She could go to London, maybe, and get something there, but her mother would never forgive her and it was hard enough to make ends meet on a stage manager salary in Plymouth, never mind London, where rent was astronomical. Connie had worked hard to get out of the village, but she'd been sucked back anyway: it was like the weight of her family was a rock thrown into the sea. She was in a rowing boat, pulling valiantly away, but the ripples were too strong and drew her in.

'How many people come to the museum in a week, anyway?' She guided her uncle to a fraying easy chair with wooden armrests and a faded poppy design behind the glass-fronted counter at the entrance to the museum; he lowered himself into it carefully.

'Thankee, maid. Not many, these days. 'Andful or more in the summer, every week. None in the winter, I usually shuts up shop from October.' He gave her a rueful smile. 'I stops the boat tours in September. 'Ard to see the caves when it's pizen dawn.'

Uncle Bill and her mother both used the Cornish slang she'd grown up with (and self-consciously dropped when she went to university). *Pizen dawn* was a way of saying *raining hard*. *Dreckly* meant *soon*, *teazy* meant someone was bad-tempered and *chacking* meant thirsty – there were plenty more she'd forgotten.

Connie jumped up onto the edge of the counter, pushing a pile of paperwork to one side. An ancient manual typewriter sat at one end of the counter and a wooden honesty box at the other.

'You don't even charge a standard admission, Uncle Bill,' she exclaimed. 'How on earth am I supposed to earn a wage from this? A handful of tourists a week dropping their spare change in here isn't enough. How did you manage, all these years?'

Her uncle took out his pipe and patted his pockets until he found a packet of tobacco. With a shaking hand, he filled the pipe.

'You're not supposed to smoke that,' Connie reminded him. He scowled at her.

'My gar, cheel. 'Tis my 'eart, I shall do what I like with it,' he reprimanded her. *Cheel* meaning child, and *my Gar*, my God. 'I owns the museum an' the boat outright. I was doin' a bit o' fishin on the side, till the doc said I 'ad to stop. Anyway, your muh' thinks you can smarten this all up. Get more people in, like, since you worked in a theatre, you know.'

Connie raised her eyebrows again. Working as a stage manager in a professional theatre wasn't exactly the same as managing a derelict smuggling museum.

'It's going to need a lot of cleaning up. And I'm going to charge admission, not whatever people want to pay.' She looked around her. 'Maybe get some more modern exhibits in. Stuff about hauntings, that kind of thing. Local mysteries. People love that kind of crap.'

'Language, maid.' Her uncle frowned. 'Aye, well, ye know best, I'm sure. Can ye still 'andle a boat?'

Connie nodded. Her dad and Bill had taken her out fishing from a young age and taught her and her brothers how to row and even sail and navigate properly. Her brothers, Kevin and Trevor, were both in the Navy now, like Uncle Bill and her dad had been. It was even more of a reason for Esther to rain guilt down on Connie with her dad gone too. *No one else is goin' ter look after me now your dad's gone,* her mum would remind Connie on a regular basis. Connie would usually remind Esther that she was as strong as an ox and twice as objectionable, but Esther would sniff and say, *That's what daughters are for, to look after their mothers,* and Connie would just have to roll her eyes and ignore it.

Sailing and fishing was one of the few things Connie actually had missed about Magpie Cove. It was so liberating, being out on a boat, with the wind in your hair and nothing but the empty horizon in front of you.

'Grand. I'll take ye out an' show ye the boat tour this week, then.' Her uncle sucked at his pipe and then coughed, wiping his hand across his mouth. 'I'll miss it, but times change.' He sighed, staring past her, into the dim museum.

Some things change, Connie thought, *but some things stay the same forever.* She didn't think Magpie Cove would ever change, and she was already thinking she'd made a terrible mistake coming back. She loved her family, but there were too many shadows here, too many stagnant memories. *I don't want to go back to who I was here,* Connie thought, desperately, but she could already feel the old Connie slipping back over her shoulders, like that old wool coat – scratchy, heavy and uncomfortable. *I can't be that person again.*

'I need some fresh air.' She jumped down from the counter, feeling like she was going to suffocate in the fug of Bill's pipe smoke and the musty air of the museum, and flung open the museum's old wooden double doors. Connie ran onto the street outside, her heart racing, straight into the man walking past.

2

'Oi! Watch where you're going!' The man rubbed his shoulder, frowning.

'Oh, goodness, I'm so sorry,' Connie breathed, mortified. 'I didn't think... I was...' she trailed off, stepping back into the shadow of the museum doorway. 'I should have looked where I was going.'

'Damn right you should.' The man, who was about her age, Connie realised, or a little older, had thick dark eyebrows which were pulled together in a scowl. 'Imagine if I'd been a little old lady or something.'

'Well, you aren't, so...' Connie crossed her arms over her chest. She'd said sorry, but this guy still seemed intent on scolding her as if she was a child. 'Accidents happen. It's Magpie Cove. It's not as if it's Times Square out here.' She gestured to the otherwise deserted high street – an optimistic term for the narrow road that housed two cafés, a small bakery, a butcher's shop, the museum and an antiques shop that she hadn't seen open in the couple of weeks she'd been home.

The young man gestured towards the butcher's shop door which had just opened to admit an elderly couple onto the street.

'You were saying?'

'Oh, what are you, the pavement police? I've said I'm sorry.' Connie bristled and turned to go back into the museum. But her uncle had shuffled to the doorway and was beaming at the man, leaning onto the brass door handle for support.

'I see you've met my niece, Alex. Connie Christie, this is Alex Gordon. From Gordon's.'

Uncle Bill said *Gordon's* like the name was supposed to mean something to Connie, but she had no idea what. She held out her hand to be polite.

'Hi.'

'Oh, morning, Bill. The prodigal actress. I remember you.' Alex Gordon shook her hand firmly, then dropped it swiftly, as if he was merely being polite for Bill's benefit. *Charming*, she thought, annoyed again.

'I'm not an actress. I'm a stage manager,' she corrected him. Why did everyone always assume that because she worked in theatre, she was an actress? There were so many other jobs one could do – costume, sound, props, catering, front of house. 'And I'm afraid I don't remember *you*.' It was a slightly rude thing to say, but this tall, glowering man had annoyed her, and it slipped out. She didn't remember him, anyway. In fact, she'd done a pretty good job of deliberately forgetting a lot of people in Magpie Cove.

'Polite as ever, I see. What're you doing here, then? Come to direct the panto? We haven't had one in years.' Alex beamed at Bill, not even looking at her. She smiled thinly.

'No, in fact, I'm taking over the museum from my uncle. His health isn't too good,' Connie retorted, wondering what the *polite as ever* crack was about. She thought about what Katharine Hepburn had said in one of her movies, though she couldn't remember quite which one. Something about everyone looking back at their childhood with a certain amount of bitterness. *Can't have been that bad, or I'd have remembered.*

Alex silently agreed, looking her up and down. *I'm not a bloody prize cow, for heaven's sake*, she thought, resenting being so obviously assessed. *Anyway, two can play at that game.* Wordlessly, she made a point of giving him the once-over in return. He was very tall and broadly built, with black stubble and an untidy, longish haircut. He wore a scruffy tartan shirt and black jeans, the rolled-back sleeves revealing a tattoo of some kind on one muscular forearm. He wore muddy green wellington boots, and there was dirt under his fingernails. *Typical farm boy*, she thought.

'You look like your mum,' he added, a smile playing around his lips. 'Not so much like you, Bill. No offence.'

Her uncle laughed, lowering himself into a plastic garden chair that he'd obviously placed outside the museum doors so that he could sit there and chat with passers-by.

'None taken, none taken. She's got the look of all the Christie women, this one. 'Er mother was a stunner when she was 'er age, same with this one. Natural Cornish beauties, always 'ave been.'

Connie blushed, extremely uncomfortable. It was like feminism had completely bypassed this remote Cornish village. Alex coughed and looked away, rubbing his beard: he was either as uncomfortable as she was at Bill's objectification of his niece, or he didn't agree at all with her uncle's description of her as a natural Cornish beauty. Either, frankly, was mortifying.

'Well, anyway, I've got to get on. Nice to see you again, Connie, and good to see you, Bill.' Alex gave them both a polite nod and lumbered off down the street.

'You said *Gordon's* like I was supposed to know what that was,' Connie murmured to her uncle, watching Alex Gordon's broad shoulders and back flex inside his rough tartan shirt as he walked. He seemed just like all the rest of the villagers she remembered from childhood, most of whom had never read a book in their lives, much less seen a play or been to an art gallery.

'Gordon's Dairy. You know, big farm up on the edge of the village. Trevor went to school with Tim, I think. They were on the hockey team together. You remember Tiny Tim.'

Connie frowned, trying to conjure the name.

'I don't know. Maybe. The tall one?'

'Aye, that's 'im. 'Ee works up at the dairy farm now with 'is dad. Married. Alex's the middle one. The youngest one's off at university, I think.'

'Right.' Connie dimly remembered Trevor's many friends from the hockey team, but she'd made an effort not to get involved with any of the farm boys as a teenager, despite her mum setting her up on a variety of blind dates she'd had no idea about until she'd walked into someone's house, thinking she was running an errand for her mum or 'just poppin' in for a cuppa' somewhere with her. Connie would then discover herself ushered into a living room with a gangly teen boy with mud on his wellies and a face full of acne, while her mum and whichever of her friends it was huddled in the kitchen, gossiping about a summer wedding.

To Esther, who had got married at nineteen, it was perfectly reasonable to try and fix up her teenage daughter with a 'nice local lad' with the intention that Connie would make nice local babies and settle down to a life of pig farming, but Connie had never wanted that, and she'd certainly never wanted a farm boy for a husband when there was a whole world out there, waiting for her, full of plays and props and interesting people, none of whom had ever had their hand up a cow's arse.

She also knew that, now she was back in Magpie Cove, she had to get used to her mum and her uncle's habits of giving her the life stories of everyone they met while they were out shopping or whatever, but it was hard going. One of the things she'd loved about living in Plymouth was the way that no one ever leaned over conspiratorially in the supermarket checkout queue without so much as a hello and whispered something like, *'Course, she's been to the doctors, 'ee says it's a lump, shame, what with 'er just losing 'er dog last month an' all.*

Connie couldn't deny that the local farms did churn out a certain type of physical specimen: all that hard manual labour, good food and clean air made boys that were fit, strong and reasonably easy on the eye. Alex Gordon certainly fell into that category.

But that was as far as it went. She couldn't imagine herself having any sort of interesting conversation with a man with dirt under his nails who probably thought women shouldn't read books, never mind read one himself.

'Well, I think that's enough for one day, Uncle Bill. Let's get you home for some lunch, shall we?'

3

It was all very well being a natural Cornish beauty – according to her mum and uncle, anyway, Connie had always thought her yellow-blond hair and blue eyes were somewhat plain – but as she steered the *Pirate Queen* into the bay, Connie realised that she'd have to cut her hair or at least braid it back next time she took the boat out. She'd forgotten what the wind could be like, out on the water.

Yet, though her hair whipping her face was pretty irritating, Connie's heart sang as the *Pirate Queen* negotiated the Cornish sea; the sun was shining, the air was full of salt spray and for the first time since she'd come back to Magpie Cove, she felt happy. Some of that feeling, she was ready to admit, was connected to the fact that she was alone on the boat. She loved her mum, but Esther could be hard work, sometimes, and talked Connie's ears off most of the day if she didn't invent an excuse to get out on her own.

Fortunately, now that Bill had given her the keys to the museum and his boat, Connie had a lot of work to do, and she was grateful for it. She was a practical person who liked having projects and tasks to tick off a list. And today, she was following Uncle Bill's tour itinerary around the local caves and coves, to make sure she could handle the boat and to get familiar with the route before she had to take any tourists out.

Some things about Magpie Cove were different through the lens of adulthood. She'd been back to visit since she'd left home for university, of course, though not as often as her mother would have liked. Her old bedroom felt smaller than it had when she'd lived there as a teenager, the beach in the cove itself seemed smaller too, and she'd noticed more non-locals around, which, in Connie's eyes, could only be a good thing: surfers, artists sketching on the beach sometimes, or up on Magpie Point, the cliffs surrounding the village.

The village itself seemed as down-at-heel as ever, though, in terms of the buildings, which were higgledy-piggledy, arranged along narrow, twisting streets. Connie supposed that some people might have found it charming, but to her it was cramped and weathered. Overlooking the cove, there were rows of Victorian terraces, built some time after the more traditional cottages such as the one she'd grown up in with its tiny windows, thick stone walls and kitchen garden.

Still, the village had a few new businesses opening up here and there. For instance, Serafina's café had been the local hub in Magpie Cove for as long as she could remember, but her mum had told her that the new owner, Serafina's son, Nathan, and a young pastry chef, Lila Bridges, now provided meals there for some of the less well off in the village on a pay-what-you-can basis. You could come to Serafina's and get a choice of hot meals every day, even if you were on the breadline, as so many were in the village – young families, elderly people living on their own; making a living in a coastal Cornish village was hard. There wasn't that much work to be had. In addition, Nathan was running a private catering business from the premises of the other café at the end of the street, which had never been open in Connie's memory. Maude's Fine Buns, the bakery, was run by a cheery woman in her mid-forties and her husband, who were often accompanied by their adorable toddler.

Also, since Magpie Cove had started to become a bit of a magnet for artists, art shows and fairs were peppering the community centre calendar more and more.

So, Magpie Cove was both smaller than she'd thought of it as a child – to Connie then, it had been the whole world – and more connected to the rest of the world than she'd expected.

She skirted the water around Magpie Point and followed the coastline into the next cove along, one that was only accessible by boat. This was known locally as Smuggler's Cove, and when you timed it right, you could dock the boat in the cove at low tide and explore a high-ceilinged cave where, legend told, smugglers had hidden their loot in days gone by. It could be tricky getting into the cove, and you had to time it just right as the currents could be fierce if you got your timing wrong, or turned into the cove too sharply. You had to take it slow and steady and at just the right angle to ride the crosscurrents safely. The smugglers had known, but even so, currents like the one around Smuggler's Cove were the reason there were so many shipwrecks around Cornwall.

Connie had planned her journey just right, and dropped the *Pirate Queen*'s anchor in the shallow water of the cove. It had been years since she'd been here, but the cave looked exactly the same. She climbed down the side of the *Pirate Queen*, untied the little rowing boat at its side and rowed it onto the white sand.

There was a thrill in finding coves and beaches around the Cornish coastline that you could only get to by boat: Smuggler's Cove had no walkway down to it from the cliff above, and the rocks around it were sheer and jagged. This was why smugglers in the past had used this particular cove to store their goods, Bill would tell her and her brothers when they were allowed to tag along on the boat in the summer holidays. He'd been a great tour guide in his day, with his deep, sonorous voice and Cornish witticisms. He'd given Connie a cheat sheet of all the facts he'd told tourists on the hour and a half boat ride, and she took it out of her anorak pocket to study.

Stop 1: Smuggler's Cove, Bill had written in his careful, childishly rounded handwriting across the top of the piece of A4 lined paper.

Row in. Take about fifteen minutes, let them take pictures if they want. Smuggler's Cove was used mostly by the Blackmore family around 1740–1770. They'd bring in mostly brandy and gin. At its peak, an estimated 500,000 gallons of French brandy per year were smuggled into Cornish coves. Robert Blackmore was the most famous of the Blackmores, and once broke into the Custom House in Penzance to take back the contraband they'd seized from him – but only what he believed was his. He had the reputation for being an 'honest' smuggler.

I doubt that, Connie thought, entering the cave. When the tide was out, you could walk all the way through to the other side, into another cove, though that one was peppered with huge grey-black slabs of granite rather than smooth sand. Inside the cave, there was a natural rock shelf running along the middle of the cave wall that looked like it always stayed dry; there were a few conveniently placed slabs that would enable someone to climb up on them to stash sacks or crates above the tide line. According to Bill's notes, this was where the Blackmores had hidden their brandy before distributing it by horse and cart through Cornwall and Devon and even beyond.

Connie walked through to the other side to stare out at the second cove. There wasn't much room to walk about there, because of the rocks, though if you really wanted to scrabble up them, you probably could and stand precariously at the top of one of them, maybe ten feet high above the sea.

At the top of the cliff there had once been a pub, in the tiny village of Morven. It had been derelict all the time Connie had known it – in fact, she and her brothers had spent one summer when she was about twelve, and they fifteen and sixteen, biking over Magpie Point to explore it. They'd heard that you could still find unopened bottles of alcohol somewhere in the grounds. They hadn't, but Trevor had terrified her on more than one occasion by riding his bike purposefully up to the edge of the cliff and braking at the last minute.

Shading her eyes from the sun and squinting upwards, she was surprised to see that the building was still there at all; she'd assumed someone would have taken it down by now, or that it would have blown away in the wind. Yet, in fact, it looked new – some major renovation seemed to have taken place, and there were new windows, a new roof and even a sign up that she couldn't read. Rather than a ruin, the pub looked like it was open for business.

Connie pulled her phone out of her pocket and took some pictures. The second cove didn't have a good walkway up the cliff either, though there were some old steps cut into the rock. However, Connie doubted they'd been used for years and only the least canny hiker or beach hunter would attempt them. If the pub was in business, it might be a good place to include in the tour, or at least point out to customers, in the event that they might like to end the tour with a nice lunch or dinner.

She walked back to the rowing boat, taking a few more pictures along the way for the updated tour website she was building, as well as investing in a new run of advertising leaflets. Uncle Bill still had a stack of his old ones at the museum, but they were pretty uninspiring, and filled with typos. Connie had decided to update everything and make it look modern and professional.

As she directed the motor boat around the next cove, Connie watched the pub get closer on the horizon. Whoever had taken it on had clearly spent a lot of money on it.

Connie guided the *Pirate Queen* into Morven's tiny harbour and tied the boat up at one of the free piers, gazing up at the pub. It was strange, because she could have sworn she remembered her mum saying something about the cliffs around Morven being a problem in the past year or so. Even when she was a kid, she remembered the cliffs crumbling away. Coastal erosion was a big problem in Cornwall, being as it was constantly being buffered and plagued by the sea, which was often fierce. But if there had been a problem, then it must have been fixed, because otherwise, who would open a pub at the edge of a cliff that wouldn't be there in five years?

She walked along the wooden pier joining the boats to the harbour side, and climbed some steps onto the old stone barrier that pointed out into the water, stopping to take some pictures of picturesque Morven for her tour website. She stopped to look at Bill's notes.

Morven – I usually make this the second stop.

When pepper was taxed heavily during the eighteenth century, it became a popular item for Cornwall's smugglers. Morven is a typical smugglers' cove and many spices and pepper from India were smuggled here in the 1700s. The entrance from the sea is narrow with jagged rocks; once inside, a smuggler's vessel would be totally hidden by the high cliffs. Legend says that smugglers once left a revenue man who was after them to drown in the cove, but sadly for them, the officer lived to tell the tale. Morven was used by the smugglers to hide contraband and transport it from the beach with a tunnel system, which supposedly once led from a cave on the beach to one of the local farms. Many houses in Morven and along the coast in this area also feature secret hiding places – secret rooms, or removable floorboards – where smugglers would hide their booty. There used to be smugglers' caves around Magpie Cove too but they're all closed off now.

It really was fascinating, all this smuggling history, Connie thought as she walked through Morven and headed up to the pub at the top of the cliff. She wondered which farm the smugglers' tunnel had run to, and where the old tunnels around Magpie Cove were – she didn't remember Bill mentioning it before. If there were, they'd be thoroughly unusable now, she supposed. Still, it was intriguing.

She imagined an immersive theatre experience, exploring

disused smugglers' caves, lit with oil lamps, where actors would play the parts of famous smugglers and tell tall tales while participants drank brandy and rum cocktails. Of course, even if the tunnels still existed, it would be way too dangerous an idea.

When she got to the pub at the top of the steep pathway, Connie paused to catch her breath. Magpie Cove had so many steep hills, that after she'd been home a week, she already felt her thighs and calves had got some of their strength back. She'd lost some of her fitness, working at the theatre, even though stage management could be a physical job, and she was always lugging props and furniture on and off stage to help out. Her actual job was about talking to actors and the director and making sure everyone understood what was needed and when, but it was one of those places where she found herself having a finger in many pies.

Up close, she could see that the pub – now she was close enough to see the sign, she could see it was called *The Lookout* – actually wasn't open yet; the sign on the door said 'Closed'. There were a couple of white vans parked in the car park, one with a sign that indicated a plumber, and one a decorator. So, it was still a work in progress.

She walked around the building, noting the improvements: it was almost unrecognisable from the ruin she remembered as a twelve-year-old. The lines of the car park parking bays were freshly painted, there was a *Welcome* sign over sturdy double doors, and a neat log store sat next to the door, suggesting that there were wood-burning fires within. The exterior was painted a fresh white, and the roof was now thatched. It might have had a thatch originally, but by the time she'd ridden up here on her bike all those years ago, none of it remained.

As she walked around the building, she saw that the new owner had laid a green lawn to the front and there were several large planters containing palm trees, with smaller matching pots containing bay and olive trees. The smell of the bay mingled pleasantly with the lilac which had been trained up the front of the building. Yet the cliff edge was as near as she remembered – perhaps nearer.

Cautiously, Connie walked to the edge of the lawn and peered past the palm trees in their vast terracotta pots. She was right: a sheer drop yawned below her, and if you didn't know it was there, she wasn't sure if a pot the size of the white vans parked at the back would save you.

'Admiring the view?' an amused voice remarked behind her, and she jumped in surprise. For a minute, the cove below opened up in front of Connie, and her head spun.

A firm hand on her shoulder pulled her back from the edge.

'Good God, woman. There's a reason those plants are there.'

Connie met Alex Gordon's eyes once more, but now any amusement had left them.

'Are you trying to ruin me before I've even opened up?'

4

'What are you doing here?' Connie demanded, pulling away from Alex's hand on her shoulder. 'And please take your hands off me. Now.'

Alex looked uncomfortable and stepped back, shoving his hands into his pockets.

'We haven't finished the garden yet. No one's supposed to be up here. Didn't you see the signs?' he grumbled.

'No,' Connie shot back, truthfully. 'I walked up from Morven on the coast path. You might want to put some signs that way if you're so bothered.'

'Oh. I thought there were some.' He glared at her, clearly suspecting she was lying.

'There weren't,' she repeated, with a too-bright smile. She hoped that he picked up she didn't mean it at all.

'This is my pub, anyway. That's what I'm doing here.' He glared at her. 'What about you?'

'Trying not to fall to my death, as it turns out. That cliff edge's a liability. You can't have people drinking near that. They'll get drunk, fall off. Never mind children, playing up here,' Connie lectured him. 'You can see there's erosion happening, all around the point up here. Why on earth did you think it would be a good idea to open a pub up here?'

'Well, not that it's any of your business, Miss Christie, but there was always a pub up here. And I've had the necessary surveys done. The council's got a management plan for the cliffs, including in front of the pub. I'm putting fences up.'

'You had a survey done, and they still let you build this?' Connie gaped at him in amazement. 'What did you do, bribe the guy?'

Alex gave her a flinty stare. 'Yeah, I bribed the council official. You got me. That's how we do things in Cornwall, isn't it? Not that you'd know.' He cocked his head to one side, not losing eye contact. 'What right do you think you've got to come up here and tell me about my business, when you couldn't leave Magpie Cove fast enough in the first place? Go back to Devon, why don't you?' he sneered. 'Think you're better than me, is that it?'

Connie was taken aback at his vitriol, but stood her ground. How had they got into an argument so quickly?

'No. I don't know you. Though this isn't exactly persuading me that I should.' She was aware that she'd put her hands on her hips and was scowling up at the man mountain that was Alex Gordon from her petite five-foot-three frame. 'In fact, I came up here to see if the pub would be a good place to recommend on my boat tour, but I definitely won't be doing that. So, thanks for helping me decide that, anyway. I don't want a lawsuit on my hands if someone comes up here on my recommendation and has a terrible accident.'

Connie spun on her heel and strode away. The rudeness of the man was unbelievable! All she'd done was point out the obvious, and he'd blown up like a volcano. That was twice now where she'd run into him and been less than impressed. To say the least.

She retraced her steps back to the coast path, relieved that this time she would be going downhill. She was aware that, as she'd squared up to all six-feet-whatever of Alex Gordon, she'd been covered in sweat and definitely had stains under her pink T-shirt sleeves. She berated herself for taking her anorak off mid-climb up the path, but it had been way too hot.

Esther hadn't actually ever tried to matchmake her with Alex Gordon, but she definitely had that type in mind for Connie.

I cannot believe that my mother thinks I've got any future at all with some bull-necked Cornish meathead like him, she thought, as she stormed along the path. *How on earth does she think I'd be happy, married to someone like that? Who only cares about Cornish things for Cornish people, churning out their meathead babies and making chutney? Does she know me at all?*

There was the sound of running feet behind her, and she turned around to see Alex Gordon jogging heavily down the dirt path.

'What?' she spat, as soon as he was close enough to hear. 'I think you made your point just now.'

He stopped running and held out her phone, said, 'You dropped this,' and turned to go.

'Oh.'

'You're welcome,' he muttered, over his shoulder, striding off up the pathway. Connie couldn't help but notice the muscles in his back against his white T-shirt as he powered up the hill, apparently effortlessly. Either he worked out a lot, or he'd spent a lot of time hefting cows on his parents' dairy farm.

Was there much need to lift cows on a farm? Perhaps not, nowadays.

She felt slightly remorseful for shouting at him; he didn't have to return her phone to her, after all. He could have just chucked it off the cliff without a second thought, which, if she was honest, she would definitely have thought about doing if she'd found his phone after he'd been such an arse to her. But he'd run after her and given it back.

'Thank you!' she called after his retreating back. It would have been a massive pain to have lost her phone, not least because she'd been taking pictures for the website on it all morning. He waved his hand at her without turning around.

Well, so much for getting to like farm boys, Connie thought, slipping her phone into her pocket. *They don't like me and I don't like them. Esther, you were dead wrong.*

Yet, despite herself, she turned around to get one more look at those powerful shoulders and the muscular back, and caught Alex Gordon looking back at her. She blushed, gave him a stupid little wave, and quickened her pace.

Okay, that was just embarrassing.

5

'In my day, it was just part and parcel of being a pretty girl,' Esther Christie tutted at her daughter as she removed the whistling kettle from the stove top. 'I used to get followed all the time. You just had to be careful, that was all. Stands to reason, boys that age can't control themselves. Men, either.' She poured the hot water into a china teapot sprigged with flowers and poured milk into two mugs.

'*Mum.* That's just totally wrong,' Connie protested, standing next to the sink. She'd come home for lunch after a morning wiping down the walls inside the museum, getting them ready to be painted. Fortunately, Bill had a long duster on a pole and by standing on a ladder she'd got rid of most of the spider webs; her arms were killing her now, though.

They'd started talking about the day's main story in the Magpie Cove gossip mill – Esther had just got off the phone to one of her cronies. One of the teenage girls in the village had started a campaign to stop sexist street harassment.

Connie shrugged and picked up the local newspaper, which was running the same story on the front.

'Good for her,' she read the article quickly. 'It's high time someone did something about it.'

'No, it isn't. Young women 'ave only got themselves to blame if they do silly things like walk 'ome alone at night,' her mother sniffed. 'I used to get Bill to walk me 'ome if we were out late, if I didn't 'ave a boyfriend, of course – an' I did, most of the time.' She smiled mistily. Connie stared at her mother, aghast.

'Come on. You must know that's an outdated idea, Mum. I should be able to walk anywhere I want without the threat of assault or intimidation. As should any girl or woman. Or anyone, come to that.'

Esther pointed at the fridge.

'There's some ham in there, get it out for me, there's a love.' She opened the bread bin and took out a white loaf. 'Mustard, if ye wants it.' Connie obeyed her mother, taking out some yellow Cornish butter in a dish too. 'That's why ye should be married off, my maid. Nice strong lad, look after yer, then ye won't have to worry about it.'

'Look, Mum. I don't need a man to look after me. All I'm saying is that... all right, I'm nice-looking, but it shouldn't mean that I should expect street harassment – or worse – because of that. If men do that, it's their fault, not mine. It's like saying if you leave a window open, you're asking to get burgled. Anyway, it's not about being pretty or not. It's about power. Men don't stalk us, or catcall us, or follow us in cars because they like us and want to get to know us. Or because of how we look. They do it because they want to intimidate us.' Connie opened the packet of ham. 'And, I might add, Mum, harassers don't care if you're married either.'

Esther tutted again.

'Come on now, my teazy maid. That sort o' thing doesn't really 'appen in Magpie Cove. She must be makin' it up for attention, this one.' Esther tapped the newspaper with her finger. 'Or, she's just bein' over-sensitive. I can't say what 'appens in Plymouth, mind.' She made a face as she said 'Plymouth', as if it was some kind of crime-ridden hell hole and not a pleasant city in Devon.

'But, Mum. I've told you. It happened to me here, when I was a teenager. Magpie Cove isn't immune to street harassment. Just the other day I was walking down the high street and some guy told me to smile,' Connie fumed. She hated being told to smile by total strangers. Like she was supposed to walk around with an inane grin on her face all day like a living Barbie, just because she was a woman.

'Well, you do 'ave a lovely smile, when you choose to use it.' Her mum tutted and sat down. 'All I'm sayin' is, I know what it's like, but it's nothin'. When I was a teenager, the lad next door used ter follow me around. Lovesick, 'ee was – your grandfather 'ad to 'ave a word with 'im in the end. It's just what comes of bein' a Christie woman. Men likes a pretty face an' yellow hair.'

In fact, the truth was that for one summer before she left for university, someone had made Connie feel unwelcome in Magpie Cove. It had started with someone standing outside their cottage at night, just to one side of the street light on the opposite side of the road. They'd stood there, enough in darkness so that Connie couldn't make out their face from her window, but in enough light so that they could definitely be seen, and watch her bedroom window, silently.

At first, it was now and again. Connie would go up to her room to get ready for bed, go to draw the curtains, and notice someone standing there. That first time, she'd frowned and pulled the curtains closed, not thinking much of it. Someone waiting for a friend, or having a cigarette, perhaps.

The second time, she'd stood at the window and stared at the figure for a full ten minutes, waiting for them to leave. They didn't, and Connie started to get spooked.

The third time, a few days later, Connie went downstairs and told her brother Kevin that there was someone outside, watching her in her bedroom. Kevin, who had been watching TV in the cottage's small lounge with his feet up on the sofa, had run out into the street, shouting, and the person had run off.

Connie had expected that to be the end of it, but it hadn't been.

Next, the notes started. Cruel notes, telling Connie she was ugly and stupid, that she thought she was so high and mighty and she'd better watch out, or more insidious notes, which were worse, somehow, saying things like, *I liked your hair yesterday* or *I watched you swimming in the cove today.*

Sometimes, she'd look over her shoulder and see someone in a hooded sweatshirt, following her. Sometimes, if she'd been out somewhere on her own, she managed to persuade Trevor or Kevin to meet her off the bus and walk her home, even though they rolled their eyes and said she was imagining things, or they were too busy playing hockey or football. But then they both went into initial training for the Navy and they were gone anyway, leaving her to walk home alone.

One night, she'd turned into the alley that was a short cut between the high street and the road that led onto hers. It was summer, but during one of those freak summer storms that came after weeks of dry, hot days, and sleet was hammering down from the slate-grey clouds that had rolled in off the sea.

She'd been hurrying along, her bag bumping against her thigh, when someone pushed her, hard, from behind.

The cobbled path underfoot was wet, and she'd slipped and fallen. Instinctively, she'd put her hands out to protect herself, and one of her hands had slipped and twisted. A deep pain had thumped in her wrist, and she felt a snap as her body weight fell on her hand.

'Not so pretty now, are you?' the person had murmured in her ear before running off down the alley, leaving Connie crouched in the rain, cradling her broken wrist.

After that, Connie hadn't wanted to leave the house. Initially, she had the excuse that her wrist was healing. But even after it was good enough for her to do normal things, Connie was scared to go out. She'd refuse to run the errands Esther wanted to send her on, to the bakery or the butcher, or take lunch out to Uncle Bill on the boat.

She'd never told her friends what had really happened; school was over, anyway, and she was going to leave the village soon. As far as everyone knew, clumsy Connie had fallen over in the rain and broken her wrist. It was an accident. Her so-called friends teased her about it, said she was accident-prone. When she reluctantly went into St Ives with them on the bus a couple of times afterwards – which Esther practically had to force her to do – they'd call after her as she walked home, down the street to her house, *Don't fall on your face again! Reckon you might need a walking stick, Connie. Do you need us to carry you home?* And she'd laughed and waved, smiling, waiting for them to turn away before the smile slipped from her face and her heart started beating hard, and she'd run home, preferring an honest accident to being followed and pushed by someone who apparently hated her.

Not so pretty now. The murmured words stayed with Connie for years, at the back of her mind, like a threat. The irony was that Connie had never considered herself pretty, or really been interested in beauty at all. While her friends were straightening their hair and talking about body moisturisers, or trying out the new make-up trends, Connie was more interested in watching old movies and reading the biographies of her favourite actresses. She wasn't a particularly girly girl, much to her mother's disappointment, and it was rare if she wore anything other than jeans and T-shirts. Yet, this person clearly perceived Connie as someone who was – what? Into their looks? Vain?

She wasn't. But even if she had been, that still would have been no reason to be attacked. Someone's appearance was nothing to do with who they were as a person. It was just genes. The actresses Connie read about had also lived with this same double-edged sword: on one hand, being a famous actress, both in days gone by but also in the industry now, demanded a certain look. Yet those lucky women who had, by a genetic fluke, been born with such desirable looks hadn't been paid the same as their male counterparts and had had to put up with daily sexist harassment – often on set.

Esther had been brought up to think that being followed and catcalled were just part of life for a girl. It was sad, more than anything, that Esther's freedom as a young woman – and now, even – had depended on the presence of a man, a family member or a husband or boyfriend, for her to be able to go out at night or do other things that were deemed unsafe alone. Connie's grandparents had both passed away when she was in her teens.

'The point is, Grandpa shouldn't have had to have a word with your next-door neighbour to make him stop following you around, and that boy's parents should have taught him to respect women,' Connie tried to keep her voice conversational, even though she was angry. 'And I hope people listen to this girl.'

Esther sighed and poured the tea.

'I know, maid.' Her mum took her hand over the table. 'I know you girls now, you got different ideas than what we 'ad. And it's good, I'm all for standin' up for yerself, really, I am. I suppose, when you get ter my age, you understand that "should" is a bit of a luxury word, my love. Should bad things 'appen? No. Should I 'ave lost your dad to cancer? No. Should I be looking forward to a nice retirement with 'im, off on a cruise ship somewhere like we dreamed of? Yes. But I didn't get those things, my love. Should is a word you use less as you get older.'

Esther cut four thick slices of crusty white bread from the loaf, spread them with the yellow butter and laid thick slices of ham on one side, then a smear of yellow mustard. ''Ere, eat your sandwich.' She pushed a plate towards Connie and watched her daughter eat, smiling. 'Anyway. Them notes was all a long time ago, my maid. Put it in the past.'

'I guess so.' Connie took a bite of the sandwich. It had been a horrible summer, but Esther was right. It was in the past, and it shouldn't worry her now.

'By the way, I know that you ran into Alex Gordon at the museum t'other day, though. Your uncle told me.' Esther sipped her tea. 'Nice-lookin' boy 'ee's grown up to be, I must say,' she remarked airily.

'I suppose so.' Connie shrugged, knowing that she'd lost the argument yet again. 'He's rude as you like, though. I went over to

Morven on the boat and found that pub he's doing up. *The Lookout*. Did you know about that?'

Esther nodded. *Of course she did*, Connie thought. There was little that went on in Magpie Cove that her mother didn't know.

'Very nice, I 'eard,' Esther remarked. 'Nice ter have a man with 'is own business, too.'

'I don't *have* Alex Gordon. Nor would I want to,' Connie replied, huffily, though the memory of Alex's muscled arms and back was difficult to put aside. 'Anyway, he was rude to me then, too. I was just pointing out to him his pub garden was unsafe, and he...' she trailed off under her mother's amused look.

'Didn't 'ee like that? Look at me, over 'ere, amazed,' she laughed. 'Not a man in the world likes to be told 'ee's wrong. Your father was the same. Still...' Esther gave her daughter a keen look. 'No 'arm in lettin' 'im see you got some backbone.'

'Mother, I have told you a million times. I am not interested in Alex Gordon, or any other country bumpkin you choose to set me up with!' Connie almost screamed in frustration. 'I don't care if he thinks I've got backbone or not. I am definitely, one hundred per cent not settling down with anyone in Magpie Cove! It's not who I am.'

'Ah, well. We'll see, my teazy maid. We'll see.' Esther smiled noncommittally and popped the last corner of her sandwich in her mouth. 'Eat yer sandwich, Connie. You'll waste away, and then no one'll want yer.'

Connie rolled her eyes, but did as she was told. If she didn't do what Esther wanted at least some of the time, life would be unbearable.

6

Even if she did say it herself, the museum looked great.

At ten in the morning on a beautiful sunny day in Magpie Cove, Connie opened the doors to the newly renovated Shipwreck and Smuggling Museum and balanced the new standees outside. She was offering two-for-the-price-of-one on admission, with free entrance for kids ten and under. She had a sign-up sheet ready for the boat tours and people could book online too on the new website.

Inside the museum, Connie had painted the walls, cleaned the display cases, got rid of some of the artefacts – she doubted that anyone was really that interested in a few dusty fish skeletons – and added in some newer displays.

Renovating a shipwreck and smuggling museum wasn't that different from painting backgrounds and curating props for a show, Connie realised. It was all a question of setting the scene so that visitors could experience Magpie Cove's history for themselves, and let the tales of wreckers and smugglers unfold around them.

Therefore, as well as the shipwrecks and the paintings of famous smugglers, Connie had added some of the Christie family history to the museum, representative of several generations that had lived in the Cove. Human history was important – it gave you a sense of the place as much as a broken oar from an old wreck.

Since she'd been home, Connie had spent her free time going through Esther's attic, initially to her mother's surprise. Connie hadn't shown that much interest in her family history before now, so Esther was delighted to show her all the old sepia photos of ancestors, looking unsmilingly into the camera and dressed in their best clothes.

Two things had caught Connie's interest: a series of diaries kept by her great-great-grandmother Biddy, and a copper cauldron – which now had a serrated green hole in the bottom – which, Esther said, Biddy and Biddy's mother had probably used in the kitchen over the fire. Nowadays, the cottage had a gas oven, but it still stood in the recess of what had been the kitchen fireplace.

Biddy's diaries were a revelation. Written from 1905, when Biddy was fifteen, to 1915, when Biddy was pregnant with her second child Mary – Connie's great-grandmother – Biddy was a keen botanist, filling her notebooks with careful drawings of the local plants, flowers and trees, and making plenty of notes of traditional herbal cures for everything from a sore throat to dropsy. It was unusual for a girl at that time, in a rural Cornish community, to be able to read and write at all, Connie had commented to her mother.

Esther had frowned in thought, picking up one of the diaries and leafing through it.

'Now that I think about it, this was about the time when the Christies lived up at the big 'ouse.' Esther had sat down gingerly on a dusty footstool after giving it a thorough dusting-off. 'See, once upon a time, there was more money. Your dad thought it was because o' smugglin', like. Back in the day... this would've been, what, early 1800s, maybe, there was a Christie fisherman then, I forget 'is name. Long John, your dad called 'im, anyway. 'Ee got lucky on the smugglin', so people thought, an' 'ee bought the big 'ouse, up the village. Not there anymore, but there's a picture 'ere somewhere.' Esther had rummaged through the aged box of photos and old bits of paperwork.

'So the family didn't always live here, in the cottage?' Connie hadn't known. She'd thought this had been the family house forever.

'No. Before the smugglin', they probably 'ad some shack that's long gone now. This place, we've 'ad it since whoever it was lost all the money. But Biddy's dad, that's your great-great-great grandfather, 'ee was still a fisherman, but 'ee was sent away to school in St Ives as a boy. They still 'ad money, years later from the smugglin' days, then. So when 'ee 'ad Biddy and her lot, 'ee made sure 'ee taught them readin' and writin'. Shame for them kids, though. You can see she was a bright spark, she would've blossomed if she'd gone ter school. Like you.' Esther had reached out and stroked Connie's long hair. 'My bright spark, you are. I'm so glad I got you 'ome at last.'

Connie had nodded, distractedly.

'Listen to this, Mum. There's this whole bit in this one about the people in the village she doesn't like. *Rosemary Connor is a hypocrite. If she'd ever read a book in her life she would know I am not a witch, I just choose to record the changes in nature and learn more about plants and their uses. Fisherman families know about nature. She is the witch. She could burn a hole through a door with one of her evil looks.*'

Esther had laughed.

'She was a one, Biddy! I remember your dad showing me those, years ago. I do remember them diaries being full o' comments about people in the village. She had a right sharp tongue, did Biddy.'

Esther hadn't minded Connie taking the diaries to display in the museum, and Connie had built a whole new area around Biddy and her journals. As a fisherman's daughter, it was still somewhat related to the museum, and Connie had taken some of her favourite passages and had them made into posters so that people could read them as they passed by. She intended to transcribe the best parts of the diaries into a book and have it for sale in the museum, too, but that was going to take a while. The diaries themselves were displayed in a case, open at some particularly compelling pages. Connie had compiled an interesting list of facts from them.

For instance, Biddy had faithfully recorded that, in 1914, her brothers Abraham and Abel had joined up to be soldiers along with eight other boys from the village.

Neither of them ever came home: both died at the battle of Passchendaele in Ypres in August 1917. On the day that Biddy learned of her brothers' deaths, her diary entry was messier than usual, and she had pressed a flower into the page. She said little, except to note that she and her mother had received a war telegram to the house, and that both boys were missing, presumed dead. Connie had carefully photographed this page and used it as the centrepiece of some other exhibits about Magpie Cove in the First and Second World Wars.

She had also added some copies of the family pictures, and enlarged one of Biddy, in which she stared fearlessly into the camera with a smile lurking at the edge of her lips. Biddy had that same Christie look: blue eyes and blond hair, hers pulled into a severe bun.

'Oooh, very nice, my love! Oooh, you're the spit of your great-great-grandmother!' Esther was the first in to the museum to inspect Connie's work. 'It looks so nice and bright! What d'you think, Bill?' she appealed to her brother who nodded approvingly.

'Looks 'ansum, maid. Yaw done a good job.' He sank into his old upholstered chair that Connie had kept next to the counter, sighing gratefully. Connie noticed how out of breath Bill was, just from walking up from the cottage two streets away, and exchanged a concerned look with her mother.

'She do look like old Biddy, don't she?' Esther placed her finger lightly under Connie's chin and tilted her face to the light. 'I never thought about it much before.'

'Mum, I don't. Uncle Bill, I really wanted you to be happy with what I've done.' Connie pulled away from her mother's hand. 'I've added in some exhibits. I hope you don't mind?'

'Course not, cheel. 'Ansum,' he repeated.

Connie had added the copper cauldron to a separate display titled 'Women's Work'. Uncle Bill had curated plenty of content in the cases and on the walls about Magpie Cove's fishermen, but nothing about the women who had kept the village alive, both during the wars when the men were away, and in normal times too. The women had always been the backbone of the community, keeping the families fed and the children looked after, but also preparing the fish for market, working on the farms up past the village and inland, and often doing building work and manual labour around the village too.

Last, Connie added a display about famous Cornish women from history, including Ann Glanville from Saltash, a champion rower of the 1800s, and Emily Hobhouse, an activist and social reformer who campaigned against the conditions inside the British camps in the Boer War and attempted to end World War One by campaigning alongside other women in Britain and Germany.

'Well, I 'ope you get some custom, 'avin done all this work.' Esther frowned, going to the door and looking out, up the street. 'There are a few more tourists, nowadays, I s'pose. 'Ave you put an advert up in the café, like I said?' She pointed to Serafina's.

'Yes, in fact, I gave Lila a whole stack of flyers to give to customers. As well as the two-for-the-price-of-one entry here, I've done the same for the boat tours for the first two weeks. It's summer. I think I'll get some interest. Plus, I've set up social media accounts for the museum, so word will get around, I hope.'

In fact, Connie was excited about reopening the museum. Once she'd got stuck in, she'd realised that there was so much she could do with the place: she had plans for themed merchandise – retro-styled T-shirts, sweatshirts, tea towels and tote bags, and then maybe stocking some books about the local area, maybe some locally made cheese and wine. The website could definitely be expanded, and once her social media accounts started to ramp up interest, she'd thought of starting a blog, interviewing locals and finding out more about the local history.

'That's wonderful, my love. I'm so proud of you.' Esther wiped a tear from her eye. 'I just wish your father and brothers were here to see what you've done.'

'Oh, Mum. Come on, don't get upset.' Connie hugged her mother and handed her a tissue. Esther had never been to any of her plays, and had never told her she was proud of any of the theatre works Connie had worked on. But the museum was something Esther understood: it was important to her, and she connected to it. Connie felt a small stab of sadness that Esther couldn't manage to relate to Connie's life outside the village: her work, was who she was, and her pride in the plays she'd helped make. Nevertheless, she did feel a little bit proud of the museum, and she found that she was excited about its potential.

Living with her mother at her age wasn't exactly ideal, but maybe Connie could make it work after all.

7

A week later, Connie was eating her breakfast – kippers in melted butter and a crusty granary roll – when Esther handed her a letter with her name on it.

'Came yesterday, but you'd gone back ter work. Forgot to give it to yer last night.' She ruffled Connie's hair as if she was six years old again and wolfing down her breakfast before going off to play on the beach with her brothers. In fact, the museum had been fairly busy, and she was due to take her first boatload of tourists out tomorrow. She'd practised the route a couple of times now and felt confident about all of it except the entry to Smuggler's Cove. It was fine, as long as you concentrated and got the right tide time. She thought she'd planned it all out well, but until she did the first tour, she just wouldn't know.

'Thanks, Mum.' Connie took it, forking some kipper into her mouth and glancing at the envelope. There was no postage mark or stamp on the envelope, but the handwriting was neat and slightly slanted to the left. She opened it and slid out the single piece of paper inside, thinking vaguely as she did so how unusual it was to get a paper letter anymore – but also that this was Magpie Cove, and everything was a little behind the times.

There was no *Dear Connie*. The note read:

Came back for more did you
Still think you're too good for us
I'm watching you

A roll of anxiety uncurled in her stomach and swept over her body. Her heart started beating fast. She read it again.

It was just like before.

Connie looked up, trying to find the words to say something to Esther, who was doing the washing up and singing under her breath with her back to her daughter.

Those other notes. She remembered them all. *You looked ugly today outside the bakery* or, *Everyone loves that golden hair of yours but it's just plain yellow like straw.* Esther would frown at them and throw them in the fire, telling Connie to forget it. If someone was jealous of her, she should ignore them.

Instinctively, Connie screwed up the letter in her fist and put it in her pocket. She didn't want to have that conversation again, even though she felt that familiar old fear settle in her chest like a fluttering bird. She pushed her breakfast to one side and stood up.

'Better get going,' she muttered, and strode out of the kitchen.

The note bothered her all day. Fortunately, it was a busy day at the museum with a large group of Americans on an organised tour of the Cornish coast, who had heard about the revamped museum from Connie's Instagram account and had made a detour from St Ives. Connie walked them around the museum, talking through everything and showing them Biddy's diaries, which they were particularly interested in. She was able to distract herself in the moment, as it was enjoyable to immerse herself in Biddy's history and talk about Magpie Cove to outsiders. Yet, when the tourists had left, Connie felt exposed and vulnerable.

At the end of the day, Connie locked the wooden double doors and checked the padlock. There was no one on the small high street but she couldn't help casting a furtive eye up and down it.

It felt different. Wrong, somehow. Like someone was watching her.

She told herself she was just being silly. She'd assumed that whoever had targeted her before couldn't still be here. It was years ago now: they would have moved away, lost interest, anything could have happened. But the note couldn't just be a coincidence.

She looked around again: she *did* feel watched. The phrase 'eyes burning into the back of her head' had never felt more real, even though it was stupid. *Don't let yourself get freaked out, just because of one note*, she berated herself, but the feeling wouldn't shift. There was a sound of breaking glass somewhere, and she jumped, dropping her keys.

She bent down to pick them up, and looked up warily. Was that someone standing in the alley between the bakery – Maude's Fine Buns – and the museum? There was no one around, and it was quiet enough for her to think she heard the sound of shoes scuffling the ground. As if someone was standing there but had stepped out of sight. She squinted in the sunlight, shading her eyes.

'Who's there?' she called out, and then felt stupid for having said anything. There was no reply; no movement. Gripping her keys in her hand with one held between her fingers like a blade, she walked up to the end of the alley and looked in, her heart beating wildly.

She saw a figure at the end of the short alley, turning off towards the beach. It was so quick that she couldn't even tell if it was a man or woman, just someone's back. She couldn't even tell if they were walking swiftly or normally – it didn't look as though they were running. She ran down the alley after them, gripping her keys in her hand. But at the end of the small walkway, there was no one nearby, and the cove lay open in front of her, with a variety of people out and about. Any one of them could have been standing in the alley. And it was quite possible that whoever had been there hadn't been watching her at all.

Connie walked along the pathway crossing the top of the cove, past the terraces on her left and the sea to her right, trying to calm down. She concentrated on her breathing, slowing it down, counting to four on the inhale and four on the exhale like she did in yoga.

She was imagining things. No one was watching her. It was all right. Nothing was wrong.

Before coming back to Magpie Cove, Connie had thought about that last summer, but had dismissed it: it was in the past, and it was over. *No one was watching her. It was all right. Nothing was wrong.*

She kept repeating reassuring phrases in her mind as she walked home, but the feeling of being watched stayed with her. Whatever her brain tried to believe, her nerves didn't accept for a second. And when she got home, she realised that the keys were still gripped in her fist.

8

Connie kept herself busy as she waited for her first boat tour customers on the *Pirate Queen*; she was a little nervous, just like she normally would be on an opening night at the theatre. As stage manager, she was responsible for everything running smoothly – it was Connie who made sure the actors were where they were supposed to be, made sure the right props were in each scene and made sure the show ran to time every night. Before the opening night of the show, stage management was all about planning and communicating – supervising rehearsals, telling cast and crew about changes from the director and writing up notices. Organising a boat tour was simple compared to all that – especially since she was the only crew member she had to worry about being in the right place at the right time.

All she had to do was remember the script.

That was the hard part. Connie wasn't a natural performer – that was why she'd chosen stage management as her role in the theatre. She loved the magic of a play; the indefinable *something* that happened when the lights went down and the curtain rose. But she'd never had any desire to be in the spotlight herself.

However, she'd practised her key points over and over again, taking inspiration from Uncle Bill's notes and making her own additions. She checked the engine over; it seemed to be running smoothly, the toilet was clean and she had drinks and snacks on board in a cool box under her seat.

Hopefully one day soon, if interest continued, Connie thought, she'd get fully booked on the tours, meaning that she'd make some good money. Today's bookings took her just under half capacity, which – when you factored in the upkeep of the boat, the drinks and snacks, and Connie's time – meant she'd just about broken even. It was all right to start with, but Connie had bigger plans, and if the theatre had taught her anything, it was that good reviews made or broke a show.

As well as setting up a scan code on some laminated notices around the boat so that customers could rate the tour on a well-known Cornish attractions website, she was offering customers the incentive of a return tour for half price if they left a review – for a limited time, of course. She hoped that, in time, the *Pirate Queen* and the museum would become some of the most highly rated holiday activities in the area.

Well, here goes nothing, she thought as she shaded her eyes from the sun, watching a man walking down the beach towards the small harbour where she sat waiting with the boat. He was followed by what looked like a family, but it was hard to make out with the sun in her eyes. It looked like it was going to be another balmy day – the summer so far had been pretty hot. Connie reminded herself that she should check everyone had sunscreen before they left. At the back of her mind, there was tension, though. She realised that she was scanning the cove for anyone wearing a hood or looking suspicious; anyone watching her. She should have felt excited, but she didn't. She was nervous.

'Good morning.' Alex Gordon pulled the front of his cap down over his eyes, which were shaded with sunglasses. 'Or, should I say, heave-ho, me hearties?'

'Oh, it's you.' Connie peered behind him to the family making its way towards her. 'I'm actually just about to head off on a tour – I think these are some of my customers.' She didn't want to sound rude, but she could do without Alex Gordon right now. She ignored his attempt at a pirate joke.

'It *is* me,' Alex agreed, standing to one side as Connie welcomed the family on board, ticking them off her list. Giving people the option to pay online was definitely paying off – she'd had two families and a single tourist book for today from a link on her Instagram page. The children, perhaps eight and ten, flitted around the boat, looking at the crystal-clear turquoise sea from the edges of the *Pirate Queen* and chattering excitedly. There was a long bench on either long side of the boat, making room for thirty passengers in all. The parents settled on one of the three benches in the middle, and Connie was pleased to see that the mother immediately got out a bottle of sun cream, beckoning to the children over to spray it on their arms and faces.

'I've been looking forward to this,' Alex added, stepping onto the ramp from the jetty to the boat. 'Can I sit anywhere?'

'Excuse me?' Connie frowned. 'Bookings only, I'm afraid. Maybe next time.' She looked past him, scanning the cove for her second family group. Perhaps Alex was one of those men who found amusement in teasing women – he probably told women in the street to smile, or blurted out 'Cheer up, love! It might never happen!' when he passed you in the supermarket. Connie hoped he'd seen the new signs that had gone up around the village – she'd seen a group of teenage girls pasting them onto lampposts and posting leaflets through doors on her way down this morning. NO TO CATCALLING, they said, in big, bold letters. STREET HARASSMENT IS A CRIMINAL OFFENCE. Clearly, the campaign Esther had been gossiping about with her friends was picking up steam.

Connie wished someone had done something like it when she was a teenager, or that she'd had the bravery to do it herself. What was nice about these girls was that they seemed to be a supportive group, which hadn't been the case for Connie, whose so-called friends at the time had made fun of her when she'd been pushed over and broke her wrist. She hadn't been particularly close to anyone then, and she realised she'd missed out on the kind of close female friendship these girls had. If she had had a close friend at the time, she could have told them what really happened that afternoon. That someone had pushed her over and whispered in her ear.

Anyway, quite why Alex had decided to come over and pester Connie on her first boat tour, she didn't know, but she wished he'd just go away. He must have been passing by on some errand and – what? – thought he'd amuse himself at her expense? Get revenge for the other week when she turned up and criticised him at the pub, perhaps. Goodness, he was annoying.

'No, I have booked. *Gordon, A.* See?' He brushed her arm, pointing to the name of the single traveller on her list. 'That's me. You've taken my money, so...' he slowly took off his sunglasses, 'here I am.'

Connie jumped involuntarily as his hand brushed her arm. He gave her a wary look.

'You okay?' he asked, mild concern in his voice.

'I'm fine. Bit nervous about taking the first tour out, if you must know. Why d'*you* want to come on it, anyway? You live here,' Connie blurted out loudly, then lowered her tone when she realised that the family of holidaymakers were looking over at her – she didn't want to make real customers think she was being rude. But *really*. Alex Gordon? This was all she needed; she was tense enough. For a brief moment, Connie wondered whether her mother had anything to do with this. It would be just like Esther to persuade Alex to take the tour and engineer a meet cute she could tell her grandchildren about for years to come.

Alex shrugged. 'Seemed like a nice thing to do on a sunny day. Anyway, you said you were taking your tour past my pub, so I thought I'd check it out. How it looks from the water. Tell your customers about the big opening next week.'

Connie could have kicked herself. For some reason, she hadn't put two and two together and guessed that *Gordon, A.* was Alex Gordon, mainly because it made absolutely no sense that Alex, a local, would want to come on a boat tour of the place he'd lived all his life. She also hadn't considered the possibility that Alex would view the tour as a way to advertise his business.

But he was right: he'd paid, so there was nothing she could do about it now except be graceful and ignore the man as much as humanly possible until the tour was over. She gave Alex a fixed smile and held out her hand towards the *Pirate Queen*.

'Fine. Find a seat. But this is my tour. It's not free advertising for *The Lookout*.'

'Of course. I'll just mention it in passing,' he said airily, walking past her and selecting a seat on one of the long benches. Connie deliberately looked away so as not to be seen noticing Alex's huge, muscular arms, barely contained under his black T-shirt, or his strong thighs that flexed as he sat down on the bench. *I wouldn't give him the satisfaction*, she thought, as she stared pointedly back at the cove, watching the rest of her customers approach the boat. She took in a deep breath and steadied herself. It was all right. This would be a good day.

The smell of the sun lotion mixed with the clear salt breeze off the water helped dissipate her worries. Sunny days on the water were some of her dearest childhood memories, and it felt good to be able to share it with others. Out on the boat, Connie felt free. As the second family got settled in their seats, and after she'd handed out life jackets, she cast off and started the engine, a bloom of excitement unfurling in her stomach. *Here we go!* she thought, still a little nervous, and turned on the wireless microphone she'd bought so that she could be heard above the *Pirate Queen*'s motor. *Come on, Connie. Let's get this show on the road*, she urged herself.

'Welcome, everybody, to the *Pirate Queen*, Cornwall's best smuggling tour! I'm Connie Christie, and we'll be exploring out-of-the-way coves and beaches and learning about Cornwall's fascinating history. Prepare to be shocked, thrilled and delighted!' She grinned, feeling an unfamiliar sensation envelop her as she continued her spiel, guiding the *Pirate Queen* out of Magpie Cove.

Was it possible that she was enjoying performing a little?

9

Connie was standing on the white sand of Smugglers' Cove, drinking a bottle of water and staring out to sea. It was such a beautiful day, and she felt as though she'd managed to leave any anxiety she might have had about the anonymous note she'd got the other day on the shore at Magpie Cove.

She was happy with how the tour had gone so far. The families were exploring the cave – Connie had timed the visit just right and the tide was out, so you could walk right through – and had asked her lots of questions on the ride so far. Despite Connie's fears that she might run out of things to say, she'd found that she was remembering all the old stories Uncle Bill and her dad had told her about smugglers with ease. In fact, there were a lot of old fairy tales and myths about the caves and the ocean she realised she knew too: tales about fishermen entranced by mermaids, of pixies – or piskies – in the caves, and even tales about the stone circles nearby, away from the coast, which her dad had told her were once girls turned to stone when they were dancing.

'Can I get one of those too?' Alex Gordon called out behind her, making a drinking gesture with his hand.

She turned around with half a smile, still thinking about her dad; he'd told her those old folk tales at bedtime sometimes. She'd always believed him. He was her dad, after all, and the most honest fisherman in Magpie Cove. When Connie had got older, her fascination for stories had morphed into her love of the theatre – and there was something in that magic of watching a play, in the dark of the theatre itself, that was a little like closing her eyes and listening to her dad's stories in the warm safety of her bedroom.

'Oh. When we get back on the boat, yes – the cool box is on there,' she explained apologetically. To visit Smugglers' Cove, she'd had to anchor the *Pirate Queen* in the small cove and use the rowing boat to ferry passengers back and forth. It had taken two separate trips to get everyone ashore this time: with full occupancy, it would take even longer. She'd have to think about that for future trips. The cool box was too big to bring down as well as the passengers – she decided to get a small, portable one to bring ashore next time. 'Sorry.'

'Ah. No worries.' Alex stood next to her, following her gaze out to sea. There was a silence. 'So...' he added. Connie looked at him expectantly.

'So...?'

'It all seems to be going well so far,' he said. 'Lovely day for it.'

'Mmm-hmm.' Connie took a drink of her water.

'You seem to be enjoying yourself,' he added. 'I didn't actually know all of that stuff you were saying, about the Blackmore family. Though my mum says we're related, somewhere down the line.' He scuffed his shoe in the sand, adjusting his cap. 'You've never been to the farm, have you?'

Connie frowned. 'No. My brother and your brother were friends, but I never got an invite,' she explained, thinking, *Nor would I want to.* Gordon's Dairy was probably lovely, but Connie's brothers hadn't been interested in her tagging along with them except when they could be persuaded to have her along on bike rides. Connie didn't have much in common with them when they were with their friends.

'Huh. I didn't think so. You know our house has got access to one of the smuggler tunnels, right? You mentioned the tunnel system, so...'

'Really?' Connie hadn't known.

'Yeah. It's not usable now, we don't think, but it's there. Door in the cellar leads down there.' He shrugged. 'Makes sense if we were related to the Blackmores.'

'Wow. I did not know that.' Connie turned her face up to his. 'Didn't you ever try to get into it when you were a kid? I would have been so curious.'

'Oh, yeah, all the time,' he laughed. Connie was reminded that Alex Gordon had a nice smile and laugh when he wasn't being humourless or annoying. 'It used to drive Mum bananas. Tim got about half an hour's walk in once, we reckon, but there was a cave-in and the fire services had to get him out. She was not pleased.'

Connie grinned, thinking of Alex's diminutive yet loud mum, Simona, who ran a hairdressing salon in town. Esther and Simona went way back, and Simona used to cut Connie's hair when she'd lived at home. In fact, considering that Simona and Esther had always been pretty friendly, it was amazing that Connie had never found herself shoved in a chintzy farmhouse front room with a young Alex Gordon as one of Esther's matchmaking efforts.

'I can imagine that you don't want to be on the wrong side of your mum if you can help it,' she conceded.

'Cornish mothers,' Alex reflected. 'Tiny but terrifying. Also, she's been trying to marry me off since I was sixteen.'

'Oh, me too. It's like their mission in life.' Connie laughed, despite herself.

'At least you escaped.' Alex shot her a wry look. 'I've always been here. She must have tried every available woman in the village, and beyond. Not you, though.'

'Hm. I wonder why?' Connie met his eyes and noticed how deep brown they were, then looked away, embarrassed. 'I mean... they were good friends. I wonder why they didn't engineer it.' She blushed. 'Not that I would have wanted them to.'

'Maybe because you were as rude then as you are now? Maybe Mum thought I could do better.'

'Well, you haven't, have you? I don't see a ring on your finger,' Connie retorted, irritated.

'You seem to think you know me, so you figure it out,' he snapped back, just as crossly.

'Well, you're big enough and ugly enough to find women for yourself now.' Connie took a gulp of water. 'You shouldn't need your mother's help. At your age.'

'Charming,' he snorted. 'I never thought looks were the issue. And aren't you living with your mum now? So, pot, kettle, black, I think.'

'Jeez. You think a lot of yourself, don't you?' Connie shot back.

Alex shrugged. 'I've got reasonable self-esteem, if that's what you mean.'

'So it would seem,' she replied archly. There was a silence until he caught her eye, and gave her an apologetic grin.

'Sorry. I didn't mean to start an argument.' He held out his hand. 'Though we always seem to end up at cross purposes. Friends, instead?'

She shook his hand and offered him her half-drunk bottle of water.

'Friends. Here. Can't have one of my customers dying of dehydration. Even the reasonable-looking ones.'

'Oh. Thanks.' He took it and drained the bottle in three easy gulps. 'Reasonable-looking, eh?'

'That's all you're getting.' Connie realised that they were flirting, suddenly. *How had that happened?* She never flirted, not with anyone – it was too easy to unwittingly give the wrong impression. Yet, somehow, it had happened without her intending it.

'I always thought you were stuck-up,' he said, suddenly. 'That's what I meant before. When we were at school. You had a bit of reputation for being rude. I remember Mum mentioning you to me, in fact, back then. And I told her I didn't like you.'

'Oh. I now take back "reasonable-looking",' she retorted, only half joking.

'No, I mean, I didn't know you, and then you left for university. You were always quiet, I s'pose. I always thought you were pretty, though.' He cleared his throat and looked down at his shoes. Connie watched in incredulity as a blush spread over Alex Gordon's ruddy cheeks. 'I lied, saying that to Mum. I did like you. I just didn't think you liked me, and I didn't want to be in some situation where they tried to match-make us, just so you could give me one of those haughty Connie Christie looks and ignore me. So that's how come it never happened.'

What? Was Alex Gordon making some kind of move on her?

'You thought I was pretty?' she repeated, not knowing if she'd heard right.

'Yeah.' He looked up, taking off his sunglasses and meeting her blue eyes with his deep brown ones. She didn't know what to say. 'I still do.'

Bloody Nora, Connie thought. *This is unexpected.*

Just then, the mother accompanying her husband and two kids on the tour came up to ask Connie a question about the cave. They were a lively family and the children had had lots of questions on the boat: fortunately, Connie had been able to answer most of them so far.

'Umm, look...' she struggled for something to say. 'I've got to...'

'Sure. No problem.' Alex waved her away, and Connie followed the woman to the cave, where the children were collecting shells.

Had Alex Gordon really just told her he fancied her? The Alex Gordon that, whenever he saw her, always ended up being rude to her? Connie felt a mixture of panic and excitement in her stomach. Now she had to get through the next two hours on the same boat as him.

This was going to be awkward.

10

Connie turned the 'Closed' sign on the door of the museum, turned the key in the padlock and stretched, yawning, in the sun-bleached street. It had been quite a busy morning, all in all, and she was ready for some lunch.

Serafina's was busy as always, but the manager, Lila, waved Connie in. She felt reasonably okay about going to the café: it was just a few doors away down the street, it was the middle of the day and she'd chatted to Lila quite a bit now.

'Connie! There's a stool at the counter,' Lila called.

Connie made her way through the busy tables to the long wooden counter which was always festooned with leaflets for pottery shows, adverts for local window cleaners, cards written out painstakingly by careful teenagers advertising their babysitting services and postcards written in to the café from ex-visitors all over the world. Serafina's had always been popular locally, but now it was gaining more and more acclaim from the growing number of tourists who had discovered the unadorned charms of Magpie Cove.

That was all down to Lila Bridges, the café manager who had helped turned Serafina's into a thriving, pay-what-you-can community café for the village.

Yet, at the same time, Lila, who had trained in a posh college in St Ives, was also passionate about passing on her patisserie skills to the locals, and Connie had heard great things about her weekly bakery school. Lila's partner, Nathan, was the son of Serafina who had started the café when Connie was too small to see over the counter. She'd died a couple of years back, Esther said. It was a shame – Connie remembered Serafina as one of the bright sparks in an otherwise dull village of gossips and dumb farmers.

The real passion and inspiration behind Serafina's Café's new lease of life lay with Lila, Nathan's partner, who had wanted to help the less fortunate members of the village. Connie knew that for as many people who might pay a pound or even less per meal, there were plenty – and the tourists too – who didn't mind paying a bit extra for a nice coffee and a crazily delicious mille-feuille if they knew it would help local people that needed it. The residents of Magpie Cove felt sure that Serafina – who had founded the café and left it to her son in her will – would have approved of the plan wholeheartedly.

Connie settled herself on a padded leather stool next to two men she didn't recognise, and caught Lila's eye.

'Thanks. You're busy!' She picked up the menu and scanned it. Every day, Lila wrote it up depending on what was in season and available. Connie got the sense that the tourists who were starting to flock to Magpie Cove in greater and greater numbers, in pursuit of its unspoilt beach, great surfing and its quaint charm, were really impressed by the café's locally and seasonally sourced food and modern social ethos. She'd certainly heard lots of good things from the people visiting the museum.

'I know. The lasagne's really good.' Lila grinned. 'What can I get you?'

'Lasagne. Yes! Sounds great. With chips. And a glass of juice or something. I'm starving.' Connie replaced the menu in its holder and looked around the café. Apparently, Nathan subsidised the café with a chichi private catering business. She wondered how much business that got, but then remembered: for every down-on-

their-luck family in Magpie Cove who had been here for generations, there were probably three rich families in the neighbouring
towns and villages who had moved down to Cornwall from
London in search of the good life – or, just bought holiday houses
here that were empty for most of the year, driving prices up so that
Cornish people couldn't afford to buy anything.

'How's tricks at the museum?' Lila turned away to a hot plate
where two large dishes of bubbling lasagne sat next to a dish of
mashed potato, a tray of fat sausages and what looked like a veggie
pasta bake. On the side part of the counter, three tall gateaux sat
imperiously on bone china stands, covered with glass domes: a
deep chocolate fudge cake with many gooey layers, a creamy carrot
cake speckled with nubbly bits of walnut and a vegan red velvet
masterpiece. Connie briefly regretted ordering a big lunch and
wondered if she could fit in a slice of cake afterwards too. There
were also oatmeal cookies, vegan brownies and a range of Danish
pastries jewelled with fruit.

'Oh, fine. Thanks.' Connie picked up the tall glass of cloudy
apple juice Lila placed on the counter in front of her and took a
long gulp. 'Thanks for letting me leave the leaflets in here. I've had
lots of people come in with them. Lots say they didn't really know
the museum was there. I guess more advertising might be needed.'

'Maybe.' Lila shrugged. 'Mind you. I'd say word of mouth was
the thing that worked for us best. Plus good online reviews. Lots of
people use those sites to plan trips. I can write down the ones we
use, if you want.'

'That would be amazing, thanks.' Connie made a mental note
of the idea. 'Anyway, the boat tours have been going well too. And
I always point everyone to the café if they haven't been already.
Makes sense to support each other.'

'Thanks! Agreed.' Lila topped up two guys at the counter with
coffee from a filter jug and wiped the counter down. 'Another
place that might be good to mention to your customers is the old
pub up on the cliff at Morven. You know it? Alex Gordon's renovated it. *The Lookout*, it's called, now. I know he's really keen to get

as many people in for the big opening soon. I know he'd appreciate you telling customers about it,' she added. 'You probably know Alex, right? Since you're actually from here, not a newbie like me?'

Connie rolled her eyes. She knew Lila had lived in the village for a couple of years now, but Magpie Cove was one of those places where you were only considered a local if you'd lived there all your life.

'I know him, yeah.'

'What? Why the eyeroll?' Lila leaned over the counter conspiratorially.

'Oh, nothing,' Connie looked away, feeling a blush come up on her cheeks. 'It's really nothing.'

'Connie Christie. Spill the beans, or I'll be forced to ask your mother,' Lila teased her. 'Look. You tell me your Alex Gordon gossip and I'll tell you mine. Deal?'

'What gossip?' Connie asked. Lila tutted.

'No, no, no. That's not how this works. Come on.'

'Oh, goodness. It's nothing. He's... I thought he was flirting with me the other day, that's all. He came on my boat tour and sort of... aghhh!' Connie did a mock scream. 'He told me he liked me. But he also seems to have spent all the other times I've seen him being really rude and unpleasant. So...' Connie shrugged. 'That's my Alex Gordon information for you. As well as the fact that he never bothered to talk to me at all when we were kids. Even when his brother and my brother were best mates,' she huffed. 'Apparently, I had a rude, haughty vibe.'

Lila set the lasagne and chips in front of Connie and handed her a knife and fork wrapped in a napkin.

'Proper Mr Darcy stuff,' she observed.

'What?' Connie had stuffed a big forkful of lasagne in her mouth and was chewing it slowly. 'Ha. This is hot.'

'Yeah. I should have mentioned that,' Lila said. 'You know. *Pride and Prejudice.* Mr Darcy's the stroppy rich guy who hates the heroine because she's outspoken and brainy. But he secretly fancies her, then he ends up saving her family's reputation later on and being a bit of a legend after all.' Lila screwed up her face, thinking. 'Anyway, I think that's how it goes. Been years since I read it.'

'Oh, right.' Connie swallowed and took a drink. 'Hmm. I don't think Alex Gordon really qualifies as a romantic hero.'

'You don't fancy him back, then?' Lila raised an eyebrow. 'Good-looking guy. He comes into the café occasionally. Brought our dairy order a few times when Geoff – that's his dad – couldn't make it. Can't say I minded.'

'No. I don't.' Connie tried not to think of the times she'd noticed his bulging biceps and wide shoulders, or the way his black hair curled around his collar. 'So what's your Alex Gordon gossip, then? *Quid pro quo, Clarice.* I told you mine.' Connie pointed at Lila with her fork.

'Jeez. It's *Pride and Prejudice*, not *Silence of the Lambs*,' Lila laughed. 'Wait, let me just let this lady pay her bill and I'll tell you.'

Lila went to the till for a few moments to deal with a customer. Connie forked some of the fat, crispy golden chips from her plate into her mouth and chewed contentedly. They were as good as her mum's chips, and that was saying something. Connie might have had reservations about coming back to Magpie Cove, but the food at home or at the café wasn't one of them. She was eating better than she had for years.

Lila returned, flipping a tea towel over her shoulder.

'So. As I was saying. I heard that Alex has a bit of *a past*.' She leaned back over the counter and lowered her voice a little. 'I guess if you haven't lived in Magpie Cove for a while, you might not have heard.'

'Heard what?' Connie frowned. 'I mean, it's possible Mum might have told me, but she's spent her life telling me stories about the village. I just tune her out.'

'Well, I heard that he was jilted at the altar, and then he stalked the woman. Had to get a restraining order. Now, I'm not one to gossip. Though, I do know that's what I'm doing now. I mean, I never used to be a gossip before I moved here. I think I've just grown into Serafina's shoes.' She grinned. 'So it's probably just as well you don't fancy him, right?'

'Wow. Just as well,' Connie agreed. 'A restraining order?' A chill ran up her back.

'That's what I heard,' Lila repeated.

Connie looked down at her plate, feeling a wave of panic cover her.

Alex had been a stalker?

She shuddered at the thought, and then had a worse one. Had Alex been behind the notes, that summer before university?

She'd never known who it was who left her the notes – or who had pushed her over that one time. What if it *was* Alex? It would explain why he kept 'accidentally' bumping into her all the time, and it would also explain why he was cold and mean one minute and telling her she was pretty the next. She'd hardly known Alex Gordon existed before she'd left Magpie Cove. Was it really possible that someone she hardly knew – he'd been in the year above her at school and they hadn't had the same friends – could have become so obsessed with her? He'd confessed that he'd always liked her. Maybe he was one of those guys who thought it was okay to harass girls. Who thought it was romantic in some kind of twisted way.

'That's what I heard,' Lila repeated. 'Mind you, I don't know Alex, so I might have it wrong. He's kind of an intense guy, though. I can imagine he'd be the type to take it hard, being jilted. So would anyone, I suppose.'

The lasagne suddenly felt claggy in Connie's mouth.

'Yeah,' she said, trying to swallow.

'You okay?' Lila looked concerned. 'Have I said something wrong?'

Connie suddenly felt like everyone in the café was watching her. Alex might walk in at any minute, and what would she do then? She was a sitting duck in the museum: he could walk in any time he wanted and he knew where she was from ten to five every day. More than that, he knew where she lived. Mind you, it wasn't exactly hard to find out where the Christie cottage was. Everybody knew where she lived, come to that.

'No. I'm okay.' Connie coughed and took a sip of her juice. 'Just something went down the wrong way, that's all.'

'Oh. Well, anyway. You should ask him, next time you see him. Let me know if you find out any more, anyway. Now that I'm the village gossip, I kind of feel like I need to know the whole story.'

'Will do,' Connie looked down at her plate. She'd totally lost her appetite. 'Anyway, I should get back to the museum.' She laid some money on the counter and got up off the stool. 'See you later.'

'But you've left half your lunch! Wasn't it good?' Lila exclaimed, looking at Connie's plate in concern. 'Did I say something to upset you?'

'No, no, it's fine.' Connie edged her way past the guys next to her at the counter and headed out of the café. 'See you later, okay?'

'See you, then,' Lila replied, sounding perturbed, but Connie just had to get out of there. She ran the few steps to the museum, unlocked the padlock and closed the doors behind her, leaving the 'Closed' sign up. She wasn't ready for people right now.

Sitting at the desk in the museum, Connie tried to control her breathing, but her heart was racing and she could feel a panic attack coming on. She hadn't had one in years, but the feeling was horribly familiar.

She gasped for breath but she just couldn't seem to catch it. A feeling of complete hopelessness overwhelmed her, and she started crying: jagged cries that she stuffed her fist in her mouth to muffle, but that just made things worse.

When the attacks came, she got a dry mouth and the breathlessness, but also a terrible feeling of doom, like she was going to die. Logically, it made no sense: of course she wasn't going to die, sitting here in a museum on her own. But that was the thing about panic attacks: they weren't logical. The part of your brain responsible for the fight or flight response was triggered, and it made you feel as though you were in mortal danger. *Run. Hide. Fight to stay alive.*

She'd been feeling so hopeful about the museum – even cautiously all right about being back in Magpie Cove – until the note had arrived. Even until today, she'd managed to brush it off in her mind as a misunderstanding, although she wasn't sure what the explanation could really be.

Yet somehow, the fact that Lila had told her that Alex Gordon had stalked someone made her panic. Just the knowledge that there was someone in the village capable of doing such a thing disturbed her. It made Connie's fears real again, just when she'd been trying to believe that those shadows were in the past.

She'd seen a university therapist in that first year away, as she came to terms with the impact of the notes, the low-level feeling of being watched and judged, and the experience of being pushed over. The therapy had helped, but now and again she'd still have a panic attack if she was feeling stressed about something.

Her therapist had told her that panic attacks tended to happen when people didn't process the trauma they were holding – after a traumatic incident, or something like bullying or bereavement – your body and brain became used to producing these panic impulses, sometimes at the smallest of threats.

Connie concentrated on her breathing. Deep breaths, in and out. *Come on,* she willed herself. *Calm down. It's okay. This will pass.* The important thing was to stay still and wait it out, she remembered. If you started walking or running around in a panic state, you might accidentally hurt yourself. Generally, her attacks had tended to last about fifteen minutes or so, though when she was having one, it felt like forever.

'Everything's okay. I'm safe.' She made herself say it out loud, like a therapist had once suggested she do when the main attack had passed and she was trying to adjust back to feeling normal. She patted her legs and arms, her face and the trunk of her body. 'Everything's okay. I'm safe,' she repeated. 'I'm here, in this moment.'

Gradually her heart rate slowed down, but she still felt like crying. Leaving Magpie Cove had removed all her triggers, and being away at university had been the fresh slate she needed: after that, she'd deliberately stayed away. Having an attack now made her feel like a failure: like she'd undone all the good work of moving away and creating a life for herself in Plymouth. Somehow, she hadn't been strong enough or good enough for it not to happen again.

The attack passed slowly, and she was able to regain her breath. Panic attacks were so traumatic, she always felt wrung out afterwards. Connie got up and started walking around the museum. Carefully, she trod circles around the display cases, counting her steps. She started to feel more normal again.

The thing was, she reasoned with herself, just because Lila had told her that Alex had taken a break-up badly didn't mean that he was stalking her, or indeed that she was being stalked at all. Yes, it was unnerving, knowing that about him, especially since she'd received a note that seemed similar to before, but she shouldn't make assumptions. She would stay away from him but see if she could find out more about what happened – maybe Lila had it all wrong.

Time to open up, she thought, bravely. *It's all right. You're safe here. It's going to be okay.*

'You can't hide in a locked museum all your life, Connie,' she said, then felt ridiculous for talking to herself out loud.

She opened the museum doors and propped them open so that the early afternoon sunshine warmed the entrance. Maude in the bakery next door waved at her, and she waved back.

See? Everything is normal, she told herself, in her mind this time. *There's nothing to worry about.*

With the sun shining, she could almost believe it was true.

11

Connie, as designated driver for the evening, had already drunk her one permitted glass of white wine and was standing at the rear of *The Lookout*'s dining room, trying to blend into the background, when there was a tap on her arm.

'Connie Christie! I thought it was you!'

She turned around to find a coiffured blonde woman, her own age, beaming at her.

'Hello...?' Connie held out her hand and the woman shook it enthusiastically.

'Hazel Goody. You must remember! We were in the same year at school,' the woman assured her in the kind of confident tone that refused argument.

In fact, now that she'd had a moment, Connie did remember Hazel: she was one of the mean girls who had spent her entire school career making other people's lives a misery. She'd been one of the so-called 'friends' that had made fun of Connie after she'd broken her wrist. In fact, Hazel had been the one who had started a rumour that Connie had broken it getting off with a boy at school. Connie searched for his name in her memory and was relieved to find that she'd forgotten it. Hazel had pretended it was all a joke, of course. That was how she operated, saying horrible things about people and then pretending it was a joke. If you 'took it the wrong way' and 'couldn't take a joke' then you were dismissed as being over-sensitive.

'Oh, hi, Hazel,' Connie said, deliberately unenthusiastic. She hoped Hazel would get the hint and go and bother someone else, but she didn't seem to notice Connie's tone.

'So good to see you! I hear you've moved back home. That happens so much now, doesn't it? People's lives don't quite work out as planned, so back to Mum and Dad's,' Hazel continued, in her loud voice. Connie wondered where her well-to-do accent had come from, as she was born and bred in Magpie Cove, the same as most people at the party.

'I wouldn't say that exactly. You're still living here, then?' Connie retaliated with a fake smile. 'Did you ever leave, or just settle for some local?'

Hazel tinkled a very fake-sounding laugh.

'Oh, no. I live in Helston now. My other half's a property developer. He worked with Alex on the refurb of this place.' She gave a simpering wave to a burly-looking man halfway across the room who sported the same designer name on his sweatshirt that was on her skimpy vest. 'There he is. My hero.'

Connie thought that if she could have got away with throwing up in her mouth a little, she would have. Who in real life referred to their partner as their *hero*? Unless the guy had recently rescued Hazel from being mauled by a crocodile, Connie felt that was a little much. Plus, she didn't fancy the crocodile's chances against Hazel anyway.

'Your hero?' Connie queried, in case she was being unfair and in fact Hazel's 'other half' had saved her from a tropical predator at some point in their courtship.

'Dave? Oh, you know. Saved me from all this...' Hazel waved her hand around, indicating everyone in the room. 'This area's nice for the tourists, but you wouldn't get me living here anymore.'

'Right.' Connie made slightly uncomfortable eye contact with a middle-aged woman who happened to be walking past at that moment and heard what Hazel had said. Out of Hazel's eye line, the woman gave Hazel a withering look. 'Well, I guess it's not so bad. Anyway, I have to be going...' she trailed off, trying to think of an excuse to walk away.

Hazel didn't pick up the cue, however, and seemed in no hurry to move on.

'Yes, it's great, living in Helston,' she continued, breezily. 'I saw your mum in the village last week and she told me all about you losing your job in the theatre. Poor old bad-luck-Connie! Just like that time with your wrist. Remember how we used to tease you about Toby Lovell, behind the bike sheds. Oh, I'm only joking!'

Unbelievable. Connie put her glass down. She didn't want to spend one more minute with this woman who had clearly not changed one iota since school.

'Well, it's been lovely chatting, Hazel, but I really have to go.' She gave her old school bully a dazzling fake smile. 'I don't get up to the dizzying heights of Helston very often, so I expect I won't see you around too much. Still, never mind.'

Not really caring about her rudeness, Connie stalked off through the crowd to the bar, where she took a glass of orange juice and drained half of it, wishing she could have something stronger. The cheek of Hazel, making that remark about her wrist! She felt all of the old anxiety flood back, and leaned against the bar for a minute, closing her eyes and taking in a few deep breaths.

'Hi, Connie!'

Connie flinched. Had Hazel followed her across the room?

'Oh, it's so good to see you again! Ellen Robb. From school?' The woman was beaming, as if Connie was some kind of movie star or something. Fortunately, it wasn't Hazel. *Who am I? Magpie Cove's answer to Katharine Hepburn?* Connie wondered, though she'd never rate herself as highly as her favourite queen of the silver screen.

'Sorry, I don't really...' Connie smiled awkwardly. She had no memory of an Ellen Robb, unlike Hazel. However, she had no doubt that Ellen was from the village – Connie knew there was a Robb family, and Ellen had a certain familiar wholesome, ruddy-cheeked look. She was also quite petite and short, just like many of the descendants of the families who had been in the village for hundreds of years. Though, Connie thought, seeing Alex Gordon on the other side of the room talking to Hazel, the Gordons obviously came from some other stock, what with Alex being well over six feet and his brother, Tim, who everyone called Tiny as a joke, was even taller.

Unlike Connie, Ellen's hair was brown and she wore it in a bob – also unlike Connie, she'd worn a flowery tea dress for the party, whereas Connie had just put on her jeans, the boots she wore on the boat and a T-shirt, just like any other day, despite Esther's disapproval. To placate her mother, she'd brushed her hair and wore it down rather than tying it up in a messy topknot. She had no desire to make herself pretty for Alex Gordon on general principle – and, moreover, she wanted to fly under the radar in general, not stand out in the hot pink Eighties cocktail dress Esther had dredged up from the back of her wardrobe and tried to make her wear.

'Oh, don't worry. I wouldn't remember me either!' Ellen trilled. 'You were two years up from me. I hung around with my sister Junie, Catherine Monk, Anna Douglas and that lot. Remember?'

'Not really. Sorry. But it's nice to see you now.' Connie adjusted her bag on her shoulder. Esther had made her bring Uncle Bill's various medicines and they were weighing her down – as well as the sandwiches in foil Esther had also made them bring, in case there wasn't any food at the party. Connie had protested that even Alex Gordon wouldn't throw a pub opening reception for the whole village without laying on any food, but Esther had been resolute: in the same way, she'd insisted that she couldn't carry any of it because she *never got a chance to use her silvery clutch bag* and Connie *surely wouldn't deprive her own mother of an opportunity to look nice at a party for once.*

Connie hadn't wanted to come to the party at all, in fact. When the invitation had dropped through the letterbox, Esther had instantly been excited – but Connie's stomach had clenched in fear at the sight of the envelope, at first fearing another note. When Esther read it aloud to her, Connie's anxiety had remained. If Alex was her stalker – if that was the word – from the past, was this all part of some twisted plan to see her again?

Rationally, she knew it probably wasn't: Alex was opening a pub and he'd been intending to open it before she'd arrived back in the village. Connie didn't want another panic attack, and she certainly didn't want to have one here, in the middle of a party attended by what looked like everyone in Magpie Cove. Esther had been firm, though: she couldn't drive, and Uncle Bill wasn't supposed to anymore. Unless Connie brought them both in Uncle Bill's ancient jeep, both of them would miss out. Connie hadn't had an attack in years, and the one that had come out of the blue the other day had really bothered her. Now, she felt paranoid about having another one.

'Nice, isn't it?' Ellen inclined her head at the pub's dining room where the reception was being held. It was a large space, light and airy, with modern steel tables and benches and lantern-type lights that hung over the tables from industrial-looking cables. Each table held a fern or other glossy green plant in a silver plant pot. Large folding-glass partitions at the end of the room opened onto the garden beyond, where Connie had wandered that day and almost fallen over the edge. She'd seen that a fence had now been added at the edge of the garden, before the trees, which was something – but because the trees masked the view, you still really wouldn't have known that there was such a steep drop just behind them.

'It's all right.' Connie shrugged. 'Bit industrial. It's Cornwall, not New York, for goodness' sake.' She rolled her eyes. Ellen looked surprised.

'Oh. I hadn't thought of that. But I can kind of see that, now you mention it,' she giggled. 'So. How come you're back in Magpie Cove?'

'Oh, you know. Came back to help with the museum,' Connie replied, briefly. At least Ellen didn't already seem to know – clearly, she hadn't been briefed by Esther in whatever press conference she'd given Hazel Goody.

'We should go for a drink sometime,' Ellen suggested, bright-eyed.

Connie looked at Ellen's full wine glass and her orange juice.

'Correct me if I'm wrong, Ellen, but I think we're having a drink together now,' she said. Ellen giggled again.

'Oooh, what am I like? I mean, another day. Now we've reconnected. We could come up here, in fact. I think they're going to do food, too.'

'Hmm.' Connie wondered how she could get away. Ellen was perfectly nice enough, but she felt so on edge that if someone coughed next to her, she would have jumped a mile and probably smashed her glass on the black slate floor. Still, it wasn't like she had any local friends, and she definitely didn't want to have to befriend Hazel out of desperation, so she forced herself to be more attentive.

'So, you live in the village?' she asked politely. 'Do you work here too, or inland?'

'Yes, up on the hill. It's one of the terraced flats?' Ellen sipped at her wine. 'I have my own craft business. I make greetings cards.'

Connie was surprised. 'Greetings cards? You do that... full time?' Her question really was, though, *how does that pay you anywhere near like a full-time salary?* but she was too polite to say it.

'Pretty much. I'm a dog walker too, sometimes,' Ellen said vaguely, and waved to a waiter who was circulating, carrying silver platers of h'ors d'oeuvres. 'Oooh. Mini burgers.'

Might as well eat while I'm here, Connie thought, putting her glass down and taking two of the burgers, biting one and then stuffing the second one into her mouth too.

'So. What do you think?' Alex Gordon touched her lightly on the arm and made her jump, gasping. Unfortunately, the two mini burgers chose that moment to get trapped in her throat, and she had to suffer the indignity of him patting her on the back repeatedly.

As soon as she could pull away, she did. She could have been wrong about Alex, but she felt uneasy around him now.

'Thanks. I'm okay.' Connie accepted a glass of water from Ellen and took a long gulp.

'It's all so lovely, Alex!' Ellen filled in the uncomfortable silence. 'Everything looks so... sparkly! I love it. I actually really like that industrial look anyway, so don't worry,' she added.

Alex frowned. 'Don't people like the décor?' He glanced around at the crowd. 'I've had nothing but compliments on it.'

'Oh, gosh, don't listen to me! What do I know?' Ellen gushed, gazing up at Alex like a hare at the moon. '*I* think it's perfectly wonderful, what you've done. I look forward to coming up here all the time.' She shot him a glance under her eyelashes that Alex couldn't fail to notice; Connie was still halfway through a choking fit and she'd divined its meaning easily enough. Ellen was flirting with Alex – not only that, she was gazing up at him as if he was some kind of king or sex god. In Connie's mind, no man deserved that – most of them already thought far too much of themselves as it was.

'Oh. Well, thanks, Ellen.' Alex looked slightly uncomfortable and turned his attention back to Connie. 'You all right now?'

'I'm fine,' Connie gasped. 'Ignore me.'

'So, how's it going at the museum? Oh, and how rude of me – can I get you ladies a top-up?' He grabbed a wine bottle from a passing waiter.

'Not for me, I'm driving.' Connie held her hand over the top of her glass.

'I'd love some more.' Ellen beamed, gulping down what remained in her glass and holding it out to be refilled.

'You're driving? That's a shame.' Alex filled Ellen's glass without taking his eyes off Connie.

'I've got to get Mum and Uncle Bill back,' she explained, clearing her throat. How could he be so... *normal*, if he really *was* stalking her? She wondered how she could ask him about his past, to see if what Lila had told her was right. But you couldn't exactly just blurt out *so, I heard your ex had to get a restraining order. Care to comment?*

'Ah. Well, at the very least, come and see the garden. I want to show you our safety precautions, since you were so bothered about them before. It would be nice if you could recommend the pub to your customers at the museum and on the boat tour.' He bowed formally and stood to one side. 'If madam would allow me. Ellen, you'll excuse us, won't you?'

He said it in such a way that didn't really invite any argument; though Connie could see Ellen looked disappointed. Connie felt sorry for her, but it was best for Ellen if she didn't get too close to Alex – if he was dangerous, after all. In fact, it would probably be the brave thing to do to move Alex away from Ellen altogether. God alone knew what someone like him might do to an innocent-seeming girl with so obvious a crush.

'It was nice to meet you, Ellen.' Connie gave Ellen a little wave. 'I'll see you around, maybe.'

'Oh. Yes, definitely!' Ellen bobbed on her toes awkwardly.

'Thank you,' Alex murmured to Connie as they walked away. 'I would have got stuck with her otherwise.'

'Who, Ellen? She seems okay.' Connie frowned. 'Unlike your friend Hazel Goody.'

'Oh, Hazel. She's harmless.' Alex rolled his eyes.

'I wouldn't say that, exactly,' Connie countered. 'You must remember what she was like at school.'

'I just remember her being kind of popular. Not the smartest, but nice enough.' Alex shrugged. 'I don't really know her that well, anyway. Dave's one of the guys I worked with on this place.'

'Ugh. Exactly what I'd expect a man to say.' Connie made a face. 'Girls are only that bitchy to each other.'

'She was bitchy? I don't remember that,' Alex insisted.

'You wouldn't. She was nice to boys she fancied.' Connie remembered Hazel back then: how she could flip from savage bully playing mind games to all sweetness and light when she wanted something from you, or if she wanted to impress a boy. She didn't doubt for a second that the old Hazel was still in there somewhere.

'Ah. Well, she's nice enough. But every time I see Ellen, she gives me these *looks*. It's embarrassing,' he muttered. 'She's a funny one.'

'What are you on about? She seemed perfectly nice to me,' Connie retorted. 'But then, I suppose you've got pretty bad judgement as far as women go.'

They'd reached the garden now and there were few people outside; it was overcast and quite windy.

'What?' Alex did a double take and stared at her. 'What's that supposed to mean?'

Connie hadn't meant to say it, but her heightened state of nervousness and potential panic had got the better of her.

'Never mind. Show me this fence you're so pleased with,' she snapped.

'No. Not until you tell me why you just said that.' He was scowling now, and his strong jaw and thick eyebrows made it worse. Still, Connie stood her ground, despite the fact that her heart had started pounding. *Don't fall apart now*, she willed herself.

'Well, it's just that...' She swallowed and took in a deep breath, 'I heard that things didn't go so well for you in the past. With women. One woman.'

He continued staring at her.

'You know what I mean.' Connie met his stare. Now she'd said it and she couldn't go back, so she might as well find out what she wanted to know.

'No. I don't. Please enlighten me.' His tone was cold now – all his previous warmth had disappeared. Connie wrapped her arms around herself against the biting wind which whipped against the cliff.

'I heard that you got jilted at the altar, and then you...' Connie wet her lips. 'She had to get a restraining order. Because you wouldn't leave her alone.' She stared up at him defiantly. 'Well? Is it true?'

Alex gave her a long look without saying anything.

'I don't know you very well, Connie, so I'm going to give you the benefit of the doubt and assume that you're just really, really bad at social interactions,' he said, his voice flat and angry. 'What right do you think you have to come to the opening of my pub, which is supposed to be a happy day, and accuse me of... what? Harassing my ex-fiancée? What would you know about it? You don't know anything about me other than some vague tittle-tattle you've picked up in the village.'

'That's just a very self-righteous way of not answering the question,' Connie shot back. Maybe it was her own experience that had put her back up. Maybe, if she hadn't been harassed all those years ago, that particular piece of gossip wouldn't have stuck in her mind about Alex and worried her. But it felt too close to home, and she was angry. Angry at the thought that Alex might have done that to another woman, and angry that, if he had, there had been moments where she thought she could have grown to like him. Worst of all, she was afraid, too, that he might have been the one that pushed her over in the alleyway all those years ago and murmured, *Not so pretty now, are you?*

She shivered at the memory.

'No, it isn't. And why do I have to answer to you, anyway? I would've thought that you, of all people, would know not to listen to gossip in the village. I thought you were different. But I see I was wrong. You seem to think you're in charge of me for some reason, yet we hardly know each other. Though what I do know makes you look like an interfering, mean-spirited, superior b—' He stopped himself saying it at the last minute, but they both knew what he'd been about to say.

An interfering, mean-spirited, superior bitch.

The words hung in the air between them. Connie took a step back, eyes wide.

'Connie, I'm sorry. I didn't mean that.' He moved towards her, but she turned and walked away, tears brimming in her eyes. Yes, she'd overstepped the line – Alex's past wasn't any of her business. But his sudden anger had really hurt.

She ran back into the reception room and outside to the front of the pub where the cars were parked, feeling the tears well up in her eyes.

Connie felt terrible. *Had* she got it so wrong? Alex was right: gossip was rife in Magpie Cove and it always had been. But he also hadn't really answered her question – although his anger was clear to see. What would it feel like if Alex Gordon decided you were 'the one', despite your feelings on the matter? What would it feel like to have that anger directed at you in a close relationship – or over a sustained period of time?

'All right, maid? What're you up to, out 'ere? You'll freeze yer bum off.' Esther tottered on her high heels out to where Connie was standing. ''Ere, I'm getting stuck in the grass now. Give me an 'and...' She held out a hand to her daughter and extricated her shoe from the lawn. Connie gauged that her mum had definitely had more than one glass of wine. 'You're not all right, are you? Whassup?' Esther peered at Connie's face. 'Come on. Tell your old mum.'

'It's nothing. I just had a bit of an argument with Alex.' Connie wiped her eyes with her sleeve.

'Alex Gordon?' Esther looked back at the party. ''Ee upset you? Do I need ter go and 'ave a word?'

'No, Mum. Leave it.' Connie just wanted to go home.

'Whass 'ee said ter yer? I won't 'ave anyone upsettin' my Connie,' Esther drawled slightly. Connie thought that she should probably get Esther home sooner rather than later; she got argumentative when she'd had a few drinks, which was almost never.

Esther gave her a long stare and stroked Connie's cheek.

'So beautiful, my little rabbit. Don't be sad, my love. 'Tis just a lovers' quarrel. 'Ee'll be back, mark my words.'

'I don't want him to come back, Mum,' Connie tried to explain. 'We're not lovers. I barely know the man. I've told you.' She refrained from telling Esther that Alex had almost called her a bitch: she wasn't sure what her tipsy mother would do in retaliation.

Esther shook her finger at her daughter.

'Mark my words,' she repeated, tipsily. 'Does 'ee no 'arm ter upset the applecart now and again. They don't like women too docile, do Cornishmen. Likes 'em teazy, like you.' She winked at Connie. Connie could never be accused of being docile, but there was being feisty and there was being suddenly, genuinely afraid when the huge man you were having an argument with started getting aggressive. It was nothing to do with being a strong woman. You could be as strong as you wanted, but in that situation, it was still scary.

'Okay, I'm taking you home now. Where's Uncle Bill?' Back inside, Connie scanned the room for her uncle and saw him sitting on one of the steel chairs, talking to a woman about his age seated next to him. They were laughing away at something, and, as she watched, Uncle Bill patted the woman's hand. Holding her mother's hand, she approached the table and smiled politely, waiting for the woman to finish talking.

'Excuse me, Uncle Bill? I've got to take Mum home, so are you ready to go too?' she asked. She really didn't want to be here any longer and risk having to talk to Alex any more.

'Eee, maid, I'll stay a bit longer if ye don't mind. I can get a lift back with Mona.' He nodded at his lady companion, who squeezed Bill's hand affectionately and glanced up at Connie.

'Don't you worry, cheel. I'll look after your nuncle,' she giggled. 'Sober as a judge, me. I don't drink, so I don't mind takin' 'im 'ome.'

'All right, then. Make sure he gets back by nine, that's when he takes his medicine.' Connie took the small paper bag of her uncle's medicine out of her bag and put it on the table between them. 'Here, actually. Take it, just in case.'

She gave them a quick smile and left them to it. It was pointless reminding Uncle Bill not to have too much to drink, and she wasn't going to cramp his style with Mona, whoever she was. For an old sailor of few words with a heart condition who smelled of tobacco, Uncle Bill did all right with the ladies, it seemed.

Connie was trying to act normal, but her heart was still racing; it was the same feeling as so many years ago. She led Esther out to the car.

There was a piece of paper tucked under the windscreen wiper; she stuffed it in her pocket and got in, keen to get away as soon as possible. She had to make herself calm down to be able to drive safely and not zoom out of there at a hundred miles an hour, but it was hard.

'Ye sure yer all right, Connie?' Esther peered at her daughter's face as they pulled out of the car park and headed down the country road to Morven.

'I'm fine, Mum. Don't fuss,' Connie muttered.

When they got home, Connie reached into her coat for the car keys that she'd slipped into the pocket, walking up the path. She brought them out with the piece of paper she'd snatched off the windscreen at the pub. Assuming it was probably an advert for window cleaning or something similar, Connie unfolded it without thinking.

'I'm off to bed, my love,' Esther yawned, kicking off her shoes and starting up the stairs.

'Goodnight, Mum,' Connie called out, distractedly, looking at what was written on the piece of paper.

Everyone says your so pretty Connie but I know your ugly

Connie drew in a breath and dropped the note on the stone

flags of the kitchen floor. She leaned against the wall, staring at the note. There could be no doubt about it now. Whoever had sent her those cruel notes, once upon a time, was sending them again. It couldn't be a coincidence: they said the same things, delivered in the same way.

But why? Why would someone do this? And why Connie?

She went to the window and looked out onto the street. There was no one there, but Connie still felt watched. Shivering, she locked the door and pulled the curtains closed.

Why couldn't whoever it was just leave her alone?

12

'Thanks so much for visiting,' Connie called after the older couple as they walked out of the museum clutching the new tote bags she'd just had delivered that morning. The museum was quiet, and she'd just sat down at the counter with the intention of designing up some souvenir mugs on her laptop when she looked up to see Alex Gordon enter.

Bloody hell, what does he want? she thought, looking back at the laptop, but she couldn't really act as though she hadn't noticed him: there was no one else in the museum apart from a mum with her young son, looking at the models of fishing boats up on the mezzanine. Plus, Alex tended to fill any space he was in with his sheer size and glowering looks.

'Morning,' he stood at the counter, hands in pockets.

Connie felt a whirl of panic begin in her stomach, but she had to remind herself they weren't alone. The mum and her son were talking quietly in the background, and the doors were open: if Alex did anything, she could shout for help. She didn't trust him, but this was her workplace. It was public: surely, no one would risk anything as obvious as walking in and – what? – dropping off an insulting note, then leaving?

She hadn't mentioned it to her mother this morning, primarily because Esther had a hangover and was still in bed, although she claimed to have caught a cold at the party. But it was also habit, not to talk about it. What would Esther say, anyway? Probably the same as always. *Someone playing silly beggars, just jealous of you, ignore it, my love.*

'Morning,' she replied, feeling nervous but determined not to show it. 'Can I help you?'

'Just passing, thought I'd pop in,' he said, looking shifty. 'See what's new.'

'Well, I don't know what to tell you, but this is a museum. So, not much new at all, I'm afraid.' She stared up at him defiantly, aware that she was overcompensating for her unease by being mean.

'Right. And how are you?'

'Fine.' Connie looked at her laptop pointedly. 'Busy.' In fact, she was only just holding it together. She'd hardly slept, imagining that someone was standing outside her bedroom window, across the street, under the street light. Where they'd once stood, all those summers ago.

'Okay, okay. Look, I came in here to apologise for how I acted at the party. I was rude, and you didn't deserve it. I'm sorry. I shouldn't have said what I said. My ex... that's still a sore point for me, I guess.' He resembled nothing so much as a repentant schoolboy in that moment, if schoolboys were six foot four, had maritime-style tattoos on their forearms and were built like a brick outhouse.

'Thanks. I appreciate that, but I should probably apologise as well. I shouldn't have said what I did. Whatever happened between you and your ex is none of my business.' She gave him a tight smile. The feeling of panic subsided slightly. Would a stalker seek her out and apologise for losing their temper, like a normal person? She didn't know. She'd deliberately avoided researching the topic once she'd got away from Magpie Cove the first time because she wanted to forget it all and move on.

All of Alex Gordon's behaviour seemed normal: it was only the fact that Lila had told her about the restraining order that had made her suspicious. Yet, because of that, she couldn't be sure of him. Someone had hand-delivered two mean spirited notes, and she'd found out that particular piece of information before the second one had arrived. Was it a coincidence?

'Friends?' He held out his hand.

'Sure.' She shook it cautiously.

Alex Gordon was local. Even if she didn't trust him, she had to find a way to live with him being around. He still hadn't told her anything about his relationship with his ex, and she had no right to ask. He could still be her stalker: it was possible. So she had to stay on guard and protect herself.

'Looking good in here,' he said, walking away from the counter and up to Connie's 'Biddy' exhibit. 'What's all this? I don't remember this from before.' He bent over to read the pages of Biddy's diary Connie had reproduced for display.

Connie followed him to the display and stood next to him, looking up at it proudly. 'My great-great-grandmother's diary.'

'Huh. Now we know where you get your feisty streak.' He gave her an amused sideways glance. '*September twelfth. Rosemary Connor is spreading rumours that she saw me having relations with Robert Weston in Connors' Field. This is a complete lie. I have left a dead mouse the cat brought in on her doorstep and some broken glass. That will teach her to spread lies about me.*' He raised his eyebrows in alarm. 'Your great-great-grandmother did not mess around.'

'No. Though it sounds like Rosemary Connor was a bit of a so-and-so.' Connie opened the glass cabinet and took out one of the diaries. The mum and son were making their way out of the museum, and that made her nervous. She didn't want to be alone with Alex. 'I think it was in this one. Biddy says they both liked the same man in the village, but Rosemary spread lies about Biddy again and she went off with him instead. I think she ended up marrying him.' Connie flicked through the pages, one eye on the double doors as her last visitors left. 'Biddy was heartbroken. She really loved him. Sam, his name was.'

'Wow. Tough times.' Alex took the diary. 'Biddy was a pretty avid diary writer for a woman of that time. We don't have anything like this from our ancestors, I don't think. I'd love it if we did.'

'Her dad taught her to read and write. He'd been to school, though she hadn't.' Connie frowned. There was a strange noise coming from the back of the museum; some kind of scratching. 'Do you hear that?'

'What?' Alex looked up from the book.

'That scratching sound. Listen, it's quite loud.'

They both listened for a moment.

'Huh. That is a weird noise.' Alex frowned and handed Connie the diary; she replaced it in the display and locked it. 'Come on.'

They walked quietly to the rear of the museum. Connie guided Alex past the back of the exhibits and into the small room where she kept all the junk she still had to clear out, plus extra bags, boxes of aged stickers that proclaimed 'I've Been to the Shipwreck and Smuggling Museum in Magpie Cove' and a couple of broken chairs.

The scratching noise was louder now. They exchanged glances. Alex pointed at the door and Connie nodded. Outside, the door led onto a small, empty courtyard. You could get to it from the alley at the side of the museum, and the back of a house rose behind the far wall. Uncle Bill had used it to store his bits and bobs, but Connie had cleared it out as a priority when she'd taken over: the back door was a fire exit and all of Uncle Bill's broken garden furniture was a hazard.

The noise did seem to be coming from the other side of the door. Her heart was pounding now and she felt a wave of panic wash over her like it had done before.

Despite her sweaty palms and racing heart, Connie held it together and padded to the door, turned the key in the lock and then pushed the door open as hard as she could. It swung back on its hinges with a loud bang.

Connie glimpsed a figure wearing black jogging bottoms and a dark hoodie. Their back was to her, and they bolted through the doorway into the alley.

'Hey! You!' Alex ran outside, chasing the person out into the alley. Connie stood in the doorway, her hand on the handle, in a cold sweat. She felt dizzy: she was breathing too fast. It was the same person as was watching her the other day: she knew it. But what did they want? And who was it?

Alex reappeared in the courtyard after a few minutes, panting.

'Couldn't catch up. They're too fast. Whoever it is, likely a kid. I could tell from behind. Not a guy. Or, if it is a guy, it's a short, wiry one. They ran fast. I could run like that when I was sixteen, but not now.'

Connie stepped out into the sunny courtyard: despite being a bright summer day, she felt cold to her bones. She wrapped her arms around herself, shivering, and half-closed the door.

Scratched on the thick maroon paint on the outside were the words:

I'M WATCHING YOU

13

'You're sure you're okay?' Alex had enveloped her in his arms as soon as he'd realised what had happened and hadn't let go. Nonetheless, he'd manoeuvred Connie back inside the museum with one arm around her shoulders, and made her sit down. She had to admit that being in Alex's strong arms was very comforting, and though her heart was still racing, she was glad he'd been there when it happened. Only when she was seated did he release her, and went to make a cup of tea in the tiny kitchenette in the back.

'I'm right here. I'm not going anywhere,' he shouted, as he made the tea. Connie tried to slow her breath down. All she could think of was, *At least I know it's not you.* It was a small comfort to know that it couldn't be Alex Gordon who had sent the notes: he'd been with her just now, after all, and she had to assume that whoever had sent the notes was the same person who had just vandalised the door outside.

He returned and handed her a chipped blue mug. Connie had had to throw out most of them; she doubted Uncle Bill had ever washed them up.

'What the hell was that all about?' Alex leaned on the counter, looking concerned.

'I don't know. Someone hates me.' Connie gulped the tea grate-fully and made a face. 'Ugh. There's a lot of sugar in this.'

'For shock. Drink it. Carefully, mind. You'll choke if you don't slow your breathing down.' Alex watched her, frowning. 'Take some deep breaths.'

She was still hyperventilating. Alex took her hands in his and breathed along with her.

'In-two-three-four-five-six,   out-two-three-four-five-six,'   he repeated, seriously, watching her face. 'Okay. That's better. Keep going.' He held her hands still, and the warmth of his grip was comforting. Gradually, Connie's breathing slowed.

'I'm okay.' She released her hands from his, feeling awkward, and took another few sips of tea. 'This tea is disgusting.'

'You must be feeling better if you're being mean to me again. Order is restored.' Alex stepped back and crossed his arms over his chest. 'So. This has happened before?'

'The panic attack? Yeah, I get them from time to time,' Connie answered vaguely, not wanting to go into detail.

'Actually, I meant our little visitor out there.' Alex indicated the back door. 'Doesn't look like any other messages have been scratched in the paint before now, unless Bill repainted it afterwards.'

'Oh. No, that's the first time. Just for me,' she added, trying to make light of it. 'I... I've had a couple of notes too. And... you'll think it sounds stupid but I thought I was being watched the other day.'

'Why would someone do that?'

'I don't know.' Connie wanted to tell him about what happened before, when she was younger, but habit kept her from saying anything. She was so used to Esther brushing it under the carpet that she had confused feelings about telling anyone, still – despite the fact that her university therapist had assured her that it wasn't normal for someone to be harassed in that way, and it was definitely okay to be upset about it.

'You should tell the police. Make a report.'

'Oh, what would they do about it?' Connie thought of Magpie Cove's three part-time police officers: one jovial middle-aged woman, Liza, who had a police dog aptly named Sleepy, and two older male officers, both close to retirement. 'Come on. They'd tell me I was just being silly.'

'Doesn't matter. You should report it, and then if anything else happens, there's a record of it,' Alex continued. 'That's criminal damage out there, as it stands.'

'Criminal damage? Really? Graffiti at best.' Connie paused. 'I'll get the door repainted, that's all.'

'Come on. Why not ask for help?' Alex frowned.

'Because,' she breathed out, purposefully slowly, 'Magpie Cove doesn't care. Look at those teenage girls flyposting the neighbourhood, trying to get someone to care about the fact they don't feel safe walking around the village. I haven't heard anyone trying to do something for them.'

'Well, I don't know about that in particular. I think most people think they're just being teens, you know. That's what teenagers do, isn't it? Make a fuss about things.'

'Maybe, but making a fuss about things that're wrong and need changing is a good thing, isn't it?' Connie countered. 'People aren't taking them seriously.'

'Hmm. Well, your family are here: you've lived here all your life. I don't get why you're so down on the place.' He looked away. Connie wondered if it felt like she'd attacked him, but it wasn't about Alex Gordon. This was deeper than that: she resented Magpie Cove, somehow, even though she also loved it. It was the place where she'd sailed around the coast with her dad and listened to his stories as she was tucked up in bed at night. But it was also the place where someone had pushed her over and whispered, *Not so pretty now, are you*, in her ear.

'What did the notes say?' he asked, quietly.

'Oh, the first one said, *Came back for more did you, Still think you're too good for us, I'm watching you.*' Connie couldn't forget it, even though she'd burned it, not wanting to have it around her.

'The second one said I was ugly. Unsigned, hand-delivered. It just makes you feel...' She shivered, remembering all the notes she'd received in the past. 'Watched. Scared.'

'God. I had no idea. You should definitely go to the police, then, now this has happened too.' Alex sounded angry. 'Someone playing silly beggars needs to be set straight. You can't just go around scratching messages on people's doors. And the notes are just... weird.' He made a face. 'I can't imagine how I'd feel if I got one.'

'I know. And I will go to the police.' Connie said it mostly to pacify him, but maybe he was right. She should definitely report this: the graffiti wasn't vague or open to interpretation, and there was no way anyone could blame her for asking for unwanted attention.

'But you're obviously upset.' Alex's voice softened. 'I hate to see you like this. I just want to help.'

'I know. And you have.' Connie looked at him properly, meeting his eyes. 'I thought...' She didn't know how to say it. *I thought it might have been you,* she continued in her mind. *But it isn't, and I'm glad.*

If she was really honest with herself, the knowledge that Alex had her best interests at heart – and had come to the museum specifically to apologise for their argument the day before – made her a little more than glad. She didn't know many other men that would swallow their pride that way. She'd dated other guys, on and off, over the years, but she could remember having some pretty big blow-ups with them here and there, and apologies had been thin on the ground from their side. It seemed that the men she'd known before didn't like to admit it when they were wrong.

Her one serious boyfriend, Sean, had been while she'd been at university. He'd studied Biology in a building on the other side of the campus to Connie's theatre course, but they'd met on Freshers' week at a drunken night out in the student bar. At first, Sean had seemed funny, intelligent and kind. They'd studied together in the library, went out with their respective groups of friends and went to the cinema together, even though Sean liked action thrillers and Connie liked arty dramas and films with strong female characters.

Yet, over time, Connie got tired of Sean belittling the things she liked, and of making fun of her theatre friends. Sean thought that theatre was a waste of time compared to science, which he thought of as the most important discipline. It was a "Mickey Mouse" course, it was worthless, and after graduation he told Connie that she'd most likely be working in a fast food joint, because, in his words, nobody gets jobs in theatre.

In the end, Connie had asked Sean that if he thought what she did was so lame, why were they together at all? He hadn't had an answer, and so they'd split up.

After that, Connie had had a few flings here and there, but in general, she stayed away from dating. All of the straight men she met seemed rather too full of themselves.

Alex seemed different.

However, she wasn't ready right now to dissect what else she might allow herself to feel for Alex Gordon now that there was, apparently, nothing standing in her way.

'What?'

'I was worried it was you. After what Lila told me. And look, you're right. It's none of my business what went on with your ex, anyway.'

'You thought I was... stalking you?' Alex's eyes widened. 'Because of what happened with Paula? Bloody hell. Why didn't you tell me to get out of here when I walked in, if you thought that?'

'Because. Look at you. If you decided to attack me, what could I do about it?' she countered, tiredly. 'Men never understand that women are polite and nice to them when we're scared because we don't know which ones of you will hurt us and which won't. Our best defence is to jolly you along and hope we're wrong.'

'But not all men are like that.' Alex frowned. 'It's not very fair to assume I'd attack you – or stalk you – just because I look the way I do, and based on some incorrect village tittle-tattle.'

'I know, Alex,' Connie sighed. 'I know it's not all men that do these things. But the thing is, how are we supposed to know which type of man you are if we don't know you? You can't blame me for thinking the worst, in the circumstances.'

'Huh. I suppose I'd never thought of it like that.' He looked thoughtful. 'Look, about my ex, Paula.'

'It's none of my business,' Connie repeated.

'I know, but I want to tell you. So you can know everything you need to about me... and know what kind of man I am. We were engaged. I loved her. She did leave me at the altar, that's true. I was cut up about it, as you can imagine. There was no warning. She seemed perfectly happy about everything before that day. Later, when I finally saw her, she said that she'd never really got over her old boyfriend and she'd rung him the night before the wedding, told him we were getting hitched. He apparently realised the error of his ways and they got back together.' Alex took a deep breath.

'Wow. That's... something.' Connie plucked at her sleeve, slightly uncomfortable that Alex was telling her all these intimate details about his personal life, but also glad.

'Yeah. I mean, in retrospect, as much as I didn't particularly enjoy standing there in that stupid top hat, having to tell a hundred of our closest friends and family that the wedding was off, I know now it was better she told me then than we'd gone through with it and I found out three years afterwards. Still, I didn't take it very well at the time. She didn't get a restraining order against me, but she threatened to get one, and I'm ashamed to say that it took that to get me to wake up. I can see now that I was acting inappropriately, but I just...' He groaned and covered his face with his hands. 'Why am I telling you this? It sounds so bad.'

'What did you do?' She was relieved that Lila had been wrong about the restraining order, at least.

'I just wanted an explanation, how she could suddenly go off with this other guy when we'd been together three years and I'd never heard anything about him before. I was still in love with her. I mean, we were literally about to get married. I turned up at his house a few times, where she was staying. I called a few times in the night when I was drunk. I was grieving.'

'That doesn't excuse anything,' Connie replied.

'I know. Believe me, I know.' He shook his head. 'I was wrong to do it. I did apologise in the end. I even wished them well. It just took me a little while to get there.'

Connie watched him carefully: his body language, the expressions on his face. He was telling the truth, and she realised that what he'd said took guts to confess. No, it wasn't a great thing to have done, but on the other hand, it didn't sound that different to a lot of break-ups she'd heard about.

'I appreciate your honesty,' she said, gently. 'As you say, at least you found out before you married her.'

'Bloody right. Dodged a bullet, though it didn't feel like it at the time, I can tell you.' He gave her a shy grin. 'Also, you should have seen the suit she made me wear. Maroon.' He raised an eyebrow. 'I should have known she had terrible taste.'

'And a matching top hat?' Connie met his eyes, and saw that friendly twinkle in them she'd seen before. 'Didn't that make you, like, seven feet tall?'

'I was literally a giant,' he agreed. They both laughed, companionably. Connie was aware that it was the first time they'd laughed together, and a warm glow spread into the cold panic that had filled her core just minutes earlier. It was just a few moments, but it felt natural – as if a bond was developing between them beyond being irritated with each other.

'Well, I'm just glad you were here. Hatless,' she replied, truthfully. She was glad. Both because she hadn't been alone when it happened, but also that now she knew Alex Gordon wasn't trying to harass her. He was genuinely here to apologise.

'Me too. The bloody cheek of it. I'm furious about it, actually. How dare anyone do that? I mean, you're a woman on her own, running a bloody smuggling museum. How much of a threat to anyone *are* you?'

'I don't know. No threat, but whoever did this obviously

doesn't see it that way.' Connie sipped the last of the sweet tea. 'People are weird.'

'They certainly are,' he replied. 'I feel like we could do with a real drink after that, though.'

'I wouldn't say no to a brandy right now,' Connie agreed. Alex gave her an uncertain look, then looked uncomfortable.

'What?' she asked.

'No, it's... Forget it. I should probably be off.' He jammed his hands in his pockets again and turned away from her.

'Alex. What is it?'

He turned back to her, looking embarrassed.

'Well, the thing is... when I came in here, I was going to say sorry for being so rude at the party, and actually... err... ask you if you fancied a drink sometime. With me.'

'You're asking me out for a drink?' Connie stared at him.

'I know. But after what just happened, I thought it was probably a bad idea. Right?' His expression was a mix of resignation and hope. 'And, particularly after I've just told you the worst thing I've ever done, I don't think you'll be rushing to take me up on the offer. Another time, maybe. I don't want to stress you out or anything, or be *that guy*. The guy that takes advantage of someone who's just had a shock. It's fine, okay? We'll do it another time, maybe. Or maybe not!' He gave her hand an awkward tap. 'Anyway, I better go.'

Connie was surprised to see a light blush cover his cheeks. *Was Alex Gordon blushing?*

'Um. No, that would be... lovely. Thanks,' Connie replied shyly. 'I know you're not *that guy*.'

'Oh. Really?' He looked genuinely surprised. 'You'll go out with me?'

'We can have a drink. It doesn't mean we have to get married.'

He gave her a startled look. 'Married?'

'I'm just pulling your leg, don't worry.' Connie blushed. What was she thinking, saying that?

'Right. Okay... well, in that case, a drink would be great.' He beamed. 'You're sure you're all right, though?'

'I will be.' Connie smiled bravely. 'Anyway, I could probably do with some distraction.'

'I'm happy to be your distraction,' Alex said, seriously, and gave her a flirtatious look under his surprisingly long black lashes. Despite herself, Connie burst out laughing. 'Too much, huh. I thought it was, but I went for it anyway,' he grinned.

'That was so cheesy.'

'Yeah. I know. Come up to the pub tomorrow night, then? We can have dinner as well.'

'Might as well eat.' Connie shrugged. 'See you then.'

'Casual dinner and drinks. And you're going to report what happened before then, right?'

'Super casual. And, yes, okay,' she agreed.

'Good. Okay, well, I'm going to walk you home, anyway. When you finish up here.' He looked at his watch. 'About an hour okay for you? I've got to run a couple of errands anyway.'

'Alex, you don't need to walk me home. I'm a grown-up,' she insisted.

'Nonsense. Wouldn't be gentlemanly if I didn't.' He planted a quick, awkward kiss on her cheek. 'See you in a bit. You'll be okay?' he repeated, concernedly.

'I'm fine. Really.' But she was secretly glad of his offer. It wasn't far to the cottage from the museum, but she still felt pretty shaken up.

Somehow, Alex had made her feel human again, despite what had just happened. If he hadn't been there, she'd still be having a panic attack. And now he'd asked her out. *How did that happen?* she wondered. Everything she'd thought about Alex Gordon so far had been wrong, and he'd proved who he really was today by chasing after her stalker – if she was being stalked, and she still wasn't sure – holding her hands, making her tea, persuading her to go to the police and being honest about his past with her. Perhaps he wasn't perfect, but he seemed... nice.

For the first time, Connie could see what Esther had always

said about the local young men: that they could be true and steady. Dare she trust that Alex might be exactly what she never believed in? A country boy with more between his ears than farming, and someone who liked her for more than her looks?

Later, at the museum's closing time, Alex tapped lightly on the thick wood of the doorframe at the entrance to the museum.

'Home time,' he called out, coming in as Connie was sweeping up. The museum had a thorough clean every week from a couple of local ladies Esther had recommended – Uncle Bill hadn't believed in cleaning, believing that dust added to the ambience – but Connie knew that tourists expected things to be clean and tidy. As well as Doris and Dotty's efforts, Connie liked to go around herself with the broom at the end of every day as well. 'Ready to go?' He watched her with a slow smile as she finished sweeping and brushed the day's detritus out of the front door, muttering an old Cornish charm under her breath.

'Hey. What was that?' Alex hopped away from Connie's broom. 'People'll think you're a witch if you go around muttering with that in your hand, you know.'

Connie deliberately brushed his heavy work boots with the broom.

'Don't mess up my floor with your muddy boots,' she scolded him. 'And it's not witchcraft. Just something mum taught me when I was little. Out, out, fairies about; clean, clean, sweep out the mean.'

'Sounds like witchcraft to me.' Alex grinned. 'Wouldn't surprise me in the least if the Christie women had some kind of magic. Eternal beauty in return for ten toads and some cat spit or something,'

Connie rested the broom against the wall behind the counter.

'Was that a compliment? I couldn't quite tell, what with the whole cat spit reference and everything.'

'It was, but I'll be more direct next time,' he replied, a pink flush covering his cheeks. Connie tried unsuccessfully to suppress a grin.

'Are you blushing?' She picked up her rucksack and slung it on her shoulder.

'No.' Alex sounded defensive, but he was smiling. 'You ready?'

'Yeah. Let me just double check the back door. You wait outside the front,' Connie directed him, making herself walk to the back door and try the handle. She didn't want to touch it: part of her imagined that it would start turning from the other side, or someone would throw it open and stand in the yard beyond like an evil spectre. *Too many films*, she scolded herself,

It was locked; she knew it was, but she had to check.

She flipped off all the lights in the museum, and shivered as darkness lowered around her. *There's nothing here. You're safe*, she told herself as she walked out – but she was thankful that Alex stood waiting for her on the street.

'All right?' He held out his hand for hers after she locked up and, instinctively, she took it. It felt oddly natural as they walked along – down the high street, through the alley and towards Connie's street.

'I'm okay.'

'Want an ice-cream?' Alex pointed to the beach; a pink and white retro-style van stood on the small road that ran up to the beach. It was a dead end, but sometimes locals parked there to walk their dogs. 'Cat's been there most weeks since last year. Not in the winter, mind. Her ice cream and waffles are awesome.'

'Sure. I could do with some sugar.' Connie had seen the truck, but had resisted getting anything from it so far. Living at home had already made her put on half a stone, what with Esther's continual baking and traditional Cornish menu of meat, creamy mashed potatoes, fried fish, pies, chips and plenty of gravy.

Connie was also happy to have an excuse to hold Alex's hand a while longer. It felt good: secure, warm, friendly. But there was also something else going on – that kind of sexy frisson that occurred when people held hands for the first time without mentioning it. There was something electric in Alex's touch, underneath its reassurance. Something between them that made her feel a little off-centre, that made a normal walk from the museum to the beach feel charged and important.

Alex greeted Cat, a woman about Connie's age and introduced them. Connie chose a rum and raisin double cone, and Alex ordered a clotted cream raspberry ripple.

'Good choices.' Cat handed them over; Alex insisted on paying, gently releasing his hand from Connie's to do so. 'Lovely day for it,' the ice cream truck owner observed.

'Have you had many people come by?' Connie asked, shielding her eyes from the low late afternoon sun.

'Oh, plenty. The weather always brings people out. Cat grinned. 'Next time, try the waffles.'

'I will.'

They said goodbye to Cat and meandered along the sand of the cove for a while, stopping to admire the beach house at one side.

'I remember that being really dilapidated,' Connie observed, running her tongue around the edge of her ice-cream. 'Someone's really made a lovely job of doing it up. I think mum did tell me about it, but I can't remember now,'

'Yeah. It's Mara Hughes' place. She and her partner Brian renovated it. In fact, that's how they met – he was looking for a renovation project, her house was falling down.'

'Brought together by bricks and mortar.' Connie gazed at the house. 'It's beautiful, anyway.'

'Yeah. It's actually a really romantic story. Mum was a friend of Mara's mother, back in the day. She's kind of taken Mara and her family under her wing since she's come back to Magpie Cove, so I know all about it.'

Alex took her hand again as they walked along.

'I wouldn't have had you down as a romantic. Want to try mine?' Connie offered him her ice cream, but he shook his head.

'No thanks. This one is more than enough.' He was halfway through his double cone. 'Why not? A romantic, that is?'

'I don't know,' Connie shrugged. 'Just... I don't think of you that way.'

'Hmm,' Alex licked his ice cream. 'I mean, we are eating ice cream on a sun dappled beach, but anyway. Challenge accepted.'

'It wasn't a challenge,' Connie rolled her eyes. 'It was just... an observation.'

'Too late,' he shot her a knowing look that made her knees go a little weak. 'I'm going to show you just how romantic I am, Connie. Be prepared.'

'All right,' she breathed, and looked up into his eyes. There was a moment when everything fell away, and it felt to Connie as if there was nothing but them in the world. She took in a deep breath. Alex leaned down and kissed her very gently, pulling away before the kiss could deepen. She wanted to grab him and kiss him again, but held back.

She cleared her throat.

'Well. That was a good start.' She was aware that her voice sounded a little wavery.

'That wasn't it, by the way,' he was still leaning in towards her; she realised his hand was touching her waist.

'It wasn't?'

'No... I mean, it was...' Connie realised that Alex too had lost his composure a little. 'It was... really nice. I just mean, I do have some romantic plans. For us. If you're interested.' He blushed again and looked at his feet. 'God, why do I always turn into an idiot around you?' he muttered.

'I don't know, but I kind of like it,' Connie replied. 'You want to watch the sea with me for a while? I find it calming, and I could do with some calm after today.'

'Okay.'

They sat on the sand and finished their ice creams as the sun lowered slowly in the sky, talking about this and that, but just enjoying each other's company.

Connie thought that whatever romantic plans Alex might have already made for them, this was pretty perfect.

14

The next day, Connie was opening the museum doors and putting out her signs when she spotted a group of teenage girls taping up some new posters. Connie noted that some of them had been ripped off the lampposts.

Before she could say anything, Hazel Goody burst out of Serafina's.

'Hey! Hey, you! What d'you think you're doing?' she yelled, swinging her designer handbag aggressively in the girls' general direction. 'That's vandalism! Stop it right now!'

The girls ran down the high street and towards Connie, laughing at the ridiculous spectacle Hazel was making of herself as she chased them in her high heels down the cobbled road.

'Careful, Hazel, you might slip,' Connie called out. She knew it was petty, but she couldn't help it – all those times Hazel had made fun of her for falling over and breaking her wrist that time were surely due a small amount of revenge. No, Hazel didn't know the real reason she'd fallen, but there was still no excuse. 'Girls. Stop in here if you like.' She waved at the teens, then stepped aside as they ran shrieking and giggling into the museum.

'Connie Christie, I hope you're not harbouring known criminals in there.' Hazel stopped, slightly out of breath, and squared up to Connie who was standing with her hands crossed over her chest in the doorway.

'I've got four teenage girls in here, if that's what you mean,' Connie replied coolly. 'Not known criminals, though. Is it really a good look, Hazel? Persecuting four teenagers for caring about their rights?'

'You saw what they were doing. Vandalising the high street with their posters.' Hazel ripped one off a nearby lamppost and returned with it in her fist. 'Rubbish. This doesn't even happen in Magpie Cove. They're just attention seeking, and they're making the place look like a rubbish tip.'

'Mmm. And you wouldn't know anything about attention seeking, would you?' Connie retorted.

'What's that supposed to mean?' Hazel demanded.

'Oh, come on. I've never met anyone who craved attention as much as you. You had to be top dog all the time at school, and you didn't care if that meant making fun of others, as long as everyone was listening to you. You were a bully when we were at school and you're a bully now. How dare you decide what these girls have and haven't experienced? How do you know if anyone in Magpie Cove has ever been shouted at on the street? Catcalled? Were you here, on the high street, every single minute of the day? Monitoring it with CCTV?' Connie glared at Hazel, who stared back haughtily but didn't reply. 'No. I thought not. Why don't you break the habit of a lifetime and leave these girls alone? And keep your nose out of what doesn't concern you. As you took pains to tell me the other day, you don't even live here.'

Hazel stepped back, as if Connie had slapped her. Connie, for her part, felt a huge rush of satisfaction at finally telling Hazel exactly what she thought of her, even if it was twelve years too late.

'I... I don't know what you mean.' Hazel gave her a hateful look. 'But you can forget us being friends now,' she cried.

'Yeah, right.' Connie rolled her eyes. 'We were never friends, Hazel. And we never will be.'

'Ugh. You always thought you were better than everyone else,'

Hazel leaned forward and hissed, her carefully made-up features clenched in rage. 'But you're not and you never were, Connie Christie.'

Connie stepped backwards instinctively. Hazel's words were eerily similar to the notes she'd had pushed under her door, both now and when she'd been a teenager herself.

'What?' she faltered, feeling Hazel's anger as if it was heat, radiating from her. 'What did you just say?'

'You heard.' Hazel sniffed, patted her hair. 'I was just being nice, trying to welcome you back to the village, but you're just as high and mighty as you always were. Maybe you should try being friends with them instead.' Hazel pointed to the girls inside the museum. 'Maybe they're more on your level. Complainers, I mean.'

'Go away, Hazel. I'd much rather be friends with people who care about more than designer handbags.' Connie closed the museum door in Hazel's face and turned away from it, taking a deep breath and letting it out slowly. She hadn't expected Hazel to say what she did, and she didn't think she'd shown how much it hurt. It was too close to the content of the notes for comfort.

Could Hazel have been the one sending them, all those years ago? And again, now? She had been a bully then, so it made sense somewhat. Connie turned around to stare at the closed museum door. It seemed unlikely that someone like Hazel would scratch 'I'M WATCHING YOU' on the back door, but it was possible, especially if she thought she and Connie had some kind of unfinished business or a continuing rivalry.

In Connie's mind, there had never been a rivalry. Hazel had been the queen bee, and everyone else either laughed along or tried not to be noticed by her.

'Oh. My. Days! That was awesome!' The teens clustered around Connie. There were four of them, all wearing various state-ment-type T-shirts and jeans.

'You really went for her. That was savage!'

'I wish I'd had my phone ready. That would have killed on TikTok.'

'I'm glad you didn't film it. You didn't, did you?' Connie asked warily. They shook their heads.

'No, worse luck.'

'Good. Look, Hazel and I just have a lot of history, that's all.' Connie took a deep breath, steadying her nerves. If Hazel was sending her notes and trying to make her feel uncomfortable in Magpie Cove, then Connie should confront her. They were both grown-ups now, and surely Connie could make her see that this kind of behaviour was unacceptable. She'd think about it later.

'She's a psycho.' One of the girls made a face.

'Hmm. Well, she shouldn't have been picking on you guys. I respect what you're doing. I'm Connie Christie, by the way. I run the museum now, and a boat tour.' Connie thought it was best to avoid gossiping about Hazel to a bunch of teenagers.

'Seren Lundy. My mum told me about your new thing in the museum, actually. Something about Women in Cornwall.' One of the girls nodded at her. 'This is Franny, Indigo and Lola.'

'Nice to meet you. Yes, I wanted to include something about women's stories in the museum as well as all the traditional fishing stuff. Have a look.' Connie walked over to Biddy's exhibit. She felt off kilter after her confrontation with Hazel, but tried to concentrate on the here and now.

'This was my great-great-grandmother. She was an avid diarist, so I've learned a lot about the village as it was then from her writing. See, you can see some pages there,' she pointed at the case. 'I think she would have approved of your campaign too.'

'Cool,' one of the other girls, Franny, said. 'We're all about celebrating women from history that made a difference.'

'Well-behaved women rarely make history, as they say,' Connie quoted. 'I was just reading this.' She picked up a biography of Katharine Hepburn she'd been reading at lunchtimes or when there was no one in the museum. 'D'you know about Katharine? She was deemed pretty badly behaved in her time by the press,

basically because she wore trousers, lived alone, refused to be a
mother and had love affairs with who she wanted. She lived life on
her terms. People said she only ever really played herself on screen,
but I don't care. I love her anyway.'

'Oh, I think I've heard of her.' Lola frowned. She had braids
and wore a flowery cropped T-shirt that said 'SMASH THE
PATRIARCHY' on top of her baggy jeans. 'She was in that film
my mum likes. With that guy. With the leopard.'

'*Bringing Up Baby*?' Connie guessed. 'Yeah, that's considered
one of her classic movies. She did lots more, though. Haven't you
guys ever seen one of her films?' She listed off a number of well-
known ones. The girls looked vague.

'Don't think so.' Seren shrugged. 'Are they good?'

'Yes! They're brilliant.' Connie looked at the museum for a
moment. She had been thinking about holding some kind of
community event there, but she hadn't known exactly what. And
then, after the graffiti, she'd put the idea aside. But these girls were
an inspiration. They weren't letting intimidation win, and neither
should she. If Hazel was responsible for the notes and even for
breaking her wrist, then Connie would have an adult conversation
with her about it. Surely, then, the problem could be solved.

'Can we leave some of these in the museum?' Seren held up
one of their leaflets. It read:

NO TO CATCALLING
STREET HARASSMENT IS A CRIMINAL OFFENCE

There was a website address at the bottom of the poster.

'Sure.' Connie took a handful from the girl. 'Good for you,
doing this. Some people really don't get how upsetting this can be.
I hope you haven't experienced it yourself too much?' She looked
at the girl with concern.

'Some. We all have, that's why we started this.'

'I'm sorry to hear that,' Connie replied. 'And I'm pretty sure
Hazel will have experienced it too. She's just got it in her head that

your posters are more of a menace than men in cars shouting at underage girls.'

'I know, right?' Franny tutted. 'Internalised misogyny.'

'Well, I don't know if it's that, exactly,' Connie said, thoughtfully. 'But a lot of people just aren't very aware of the facts. A lot of time they just revert to assumptions and generalisations they've heard other people say. And Hazel...' she trailed off. *Hazel has a mean streak*, she thought.

'Anyway, listen. I've been thinking about holding some kind of event for the community at the museum – a kind of welcome thing, now that I've taken over. What about if we have a film night – a Katharine Hepburn movie – and you guys could do a presentation as well, about street harassment? And I could introduce the new exhibit as well maybe.'

'Sounds good,' Seren said; the other girls exchanged smiles and nods. 'You'd do that for us?'

'Of course.' Connie felt a blossoming of pride in her chest. Here was something good she could do. It might not magically erase the harassment she had experienced, but it was something. And if anyone came away from a Katharine Hepburn movie feeling empowered – or from listening to these passionate young girls trying to improve the world they lived in – then that was surely a good thing.

The Hazel problem was something she would think about later.

15

Constable Chalmers ushered Connie into a rather dusty office and cleared some magazines off the beige seat facing the desk.

'Come in, come in.' He fussed around her like a hen. 'Sorry, been meanin' to 'ave a clear-up in 'ere. Don't know where the time goes.' He pushed a pile of paperwork on the old-fashioned, baize-topped writing desk to one side, and in doing so, spilled a cup of tea that looked like it had been there a while. 'Oh, drat,' he tutted. 'S'cuse me while I gets a cloth. Make you one?' He tapped his finger on the mug.

'Umm... okay. Tea, thanks. No sugar.'

'Right you are.'

The constable pottered in a little annexe off the office which had an old-style serving hatch in the wall, meaning that Connie could see his head and shoulders as he filled up the kettle with water and selected a couple of mugs from a cupboard.

''Ow's your mum gettin' on?' the constable called out as he dropped tea bags into mugs and poured hot water from the kettle. ''Aven't seen 'er around as much as usual.'

He came in and placed a mug of strong, orangey-brown tea in front of Connie on the cluttered desk.

'Oh, she's fine, thanks. She's busy looking after my uncle Bill – and I suppose me – a bit as well.' Connie smiled ruefully.

'Ah. You might tell 'er that I was askin' after 'er. We usually see Esther in the pub for bingo on a Thursday night, and she's missed the last two.' He cleared his throat. 'Not that I missed 'er in particular, like. I mean, on behalf of all of us at the bingo,' he added, the tips of his ears going red.

'I will, Constable Chalmers.' Connie wondered if the constable had a crush on her mum. In a way, she hoped he did: Esther had been single a long time now. She could do with some company apart from Uncle Bill.

'Call me Adrian, please. So, you enjoyin' bein back in the village?' He settled back on his chair behind the desk and sipped from his mug, looking keenly at her through his bifocals.

'Umm... it's okay. That's kind of what I came to talk to you about.' Connie fidgeted in her seat. 'I had some criminal damage happen at the museum.' She gripped her mug tightly. Despite the fact that Magpie Cove's police station was hardly a tough city crime-fighting hub, she was still nervous.

'Oh dear, oh dear.' Adrian frowned and set down his mug on a tatty blotter. 'Hang on, let me get a pen, 'ere.'

He selected a biro from a jam jar of pens and pencils on the desk and held up his finger to indicate Connie should wait. ''Ang on, my love. The pad's in 'ere somewhere.' He opened a drawer on his side of the desk and rummaged in it for a few moments. 'Aha,' he grunted, taking out a pad of forms and peering at it close up. 'Right. Now we're cookin' with gas. Tell me what 'appened, an' I can write down your statement as you say it, then you can 'ave a look and change anythin' you want, then I'll type it up.'

'Okay. Then what will happen?' Connie asked, still nervous.

'We'll come an' 'ave a look at it an' see what we can do. Thing is, with criminal damage, it's 'ard to find the buggers what did it unless you get 'old of 'em at the time. More than anythin', most of what we do is statements for the insurance company. Still, you tell me what's what, and we'll take it from there.' He gave her a warm smile. 'Don't be nervous, my love. 'Appens to the best of us.'

Connie took in a deep breath. It wasn't so much reporting the graffiti that was bothering her: it was the prospect of talking about the harassment she'd been experiencing. She could just report the damage at the museum and let that be the end of it, or she could risk the constable brushing off the rest of what had happened to her in the same way that her mum did: that it was just someone being jealous and she should ignore it.

No, she berated herself. *Say everything now, and then it's done, at least.* Like Alex said, if the harassment was recorded, then if something worse happened, no one could accuse her of not having said something sooner. She hated the fact that the law worked like that: in a way, if someone was too scared to report a crime – especially something like domestic abuse or stalking – then there was that inference that the victim should have done more to prevent it when the worst happened. Whereas, in fact, the only person at fault was the perpetrator.

'Okay. But there are a few other things I need to tell you, too.'

Adrian nodded, his pen hovering over the page.

'Whenever you're ready, Connie,' he said, kindly. 'Whatever you tells me, remember I'm 'ere to 'elp.'

16

'Connie! Over here.'

Connie recognised the young woman waving at her from a table at the other side of Serafina's: it was that girl from the party, Ellen Robb. She smiled noncommittally.

'It's Ellen! Ellen Robb!' the woman called, getting up and waving more furiously. Connie waved back timidly and took her takeaway coffee from Lila's new assistant, intending to leave quickly, but Ellen got up and stood in the gap between the queue at the counter and the tables.

'Hi, Ellen.' Connie halted, unable to get past her.

'Coffee break?' Ellen asked, bright-eyed as before. Connie agreed.

'Just heading back. Can't leave the museum closed for long,' she said. She'd opened up late as it was, having been to the police station first thing. Ellen seemed nice enough, but there was something in her over-friendliness that put Connie on edge.

'Right. It was so nice to see you at the party,' Ellen continued, blissfully unaware of Connie's rather obvious hint. 'Lovely, wasn't it? The speeches were very moving, I thought.'

'Oh, right. Actually, I left before then,' Connie replied, a little shortly. 'Had to get my mum home. She was a bit the worse for wear.'

'Oh, what a shame,' Ellen cooed, looking curiously at Connie. 'You missed Alex's speech, then. It was very interesting. What inspired him to reopen the pub up on Morven Head. He's dreamy, isn't he?' Ellen sighed theatrically. 'Always had a bit of a crush on Alex Gordon, me.'

'Have you?' Connie tried to sound disinterested, though she had of course agreed to go on a date with Alex later. Still, she wasn't about to tell Ellen that. She hardly knew the girl, and her natural instinct was to be secretive about her personal life – perhaps as a result of living with Esther, an avid gossip, all her life. 'Well, I do really have to get back,' Connie smiled and tried to edge past Ellen, but the other girl stood firm.

'I've always wanted to ask him out, but been too shy,' Ellen added, still standing in Connie's way. 'Between you and me, I was trying to get my nerve up just now to ask him out, but then I thought there might be something going on between you and him. You disappeared off into the garden at the party. Very cosy, I might add. Mind you, it did look from where I was standing like you might have had a bit of a barny.' Ellen stroked Connie's arm, which was a bit more familiarity than Connie was really ready for. She flinched, instinctively. 'Poor you! He is gorgeous but he does look like he's got a bit of a temper.'

Connie frowned. What was going on here, exactly? She wasn't sure what Ellen wanted from her, but if it was gossip, she was asking the wrong girl.

'I have always liked Alex, but I'm probably just being a bit silly. He'd never be interested in me,' Ellen remarked.

'Oh, I'm sure that's not true,' Connie replied vaguely, not wanting to be drawn into the conversation.

'Don't you believe it. Connie Christie's back in town. Lock up your sons, and all that.' Ellen sniffed, then gave Connie a generous smile. 'Still, you can't help being gorgeous, can you?' She reached forward and took a strand of Connie's golden-blond hair between her fingers. It was another overly familiar gesture, and Connie pulled away, feeling uncomfortable.

She hardly knew this girl, but Ellen seemed to have some very definite ideas about her. The idea of anyone 'locking up their sons' on her account would be hilarious if it wasn't also oddly threatening, given the fact that Connie believed she might have a stalker. If anyone wanted locking up, it was whoever had scratched their message on the museum door. Connie still couldn't quite believe it might be Hazel, but she'd decided that the next time she saw her, she was going to ask Hazel, straight up, if she had been the one leaving the notes. One way or another, they were going to have it out.

'Right...' Connie managed to edge past Ellen. 'Well, you take care. Sorry, I do really need to get back. Can't not be open for the tourists.' She didn't quite know what to say – it was a weird conversation, really, and she still didn't know what to make of Ellen. But she didn't want to be rude, and she certainly didn't want to talk about Alex either. It was too new: she didn't quite know how she felt about him yet.

'Actually, I'll walk out with you.' Ellen went back to the table where she'd left her coat and bag. 'I should head back anyway. Work to do.'

Okayyyy... Connie thought, making her way to the door. For some reason, Ellen had clearly decided that she wanted to be friends, and she didn't seem like the sort of person who would take no for an answer.

Ellen trotted out of the café after Connie. 'So, you know, we have something in common.'

'Oh?' Connie asked politely, not really interested. There was something about Ellen she wasn't sure of, though she couldn't exactly say what it was. The unsolicited touching didn't help, although she realised that she was probably more sensitive to it than other people. 'So, you live this way?' she added, pointing down the street, past the museum a few yards away. Most of the houses were the other way, up the high street and away from the cove. 'Oh, right. The terraces. I remember.'

'Yeah,' Ellen said, vaguely. 'No, the thing I was going to tell you was, we've got history! Well. We haven't, exactly, but you know you've got that exhibition in the museum? Based on your great-grandmother's diary?'

'Great-great grandmother. Yes,' Connie stopped in front of the museum and reached into her pocket for the keys with her free hand.

'Well, my great-great grandmother was Rosemary Connor. Your Biddy talks about her here and there. In her notebook.' Ellen made a *tah-dah* motion with her hands. 'What about that?'

Connie frowned, opening the museum doors. 'I didn't know you'd been in to see the exhibition.'

'Oh, yes. Before the party, so we hadn't met then. You probably don't remember me. Well, you didn't at the party!' Ellen laughed; it sounded forced.

'Oh right.' Connie walked in and placed her takeaway coffee on the counter and the keys back in her pocket. She was still pretty on edge, being in the museum on her own after the graffiti incident.

At least she'd done the right thing in reporting it.

'Yes, so Rosemary and Biddy had a bit of a rivalry, it would seem,' Ellen continued, going over to the glass cabinet that held Biddy's diaries. 'My dad told us all about it. You know, the things that tend to get passed down. She and my great-great-grandfather Sam owned an apothecary in the village for some years. A chemist's, I suppose. We've still got some of their old things. They're quite nice, really, those funny old bottles with Latin names of plants and things on.'

'Oh, I can believe it. We were always looking for things like that for props when I worked in the theatre.' Connie felt a pang of homesickness for her old job for a moment: she missed the cama-raderie, the interesting projects she'd worked on – even the actors. She missed her friends too, back in Plymouth – they kept in touch with messaging and the occasional chat on the phone, but it wasn't the same. It was hard not having any real friends in Magpie Cove: perhaps that was why she found herself letting her guard down with Ellen a little. 'But, wow, I had no idea. So you're a Connor, then? They definitely hated each other, you know. Biddy and Rosemary.' She followed Ellen to stand in front of the display. 'Biddy was in love with Sam, and she lost out to Rosemary. Must've been hard for her.'

'It certainly must have,' Ellen mused, looking up at the poster that featured an enlarged excerpt from Biddy's diary. 'But, in a funny kind of way, it's nice that we can be friends now, isn't it? Put that old animosity to bed.'

'I suppose so,' Connie agreed. She wondered what Biddy would think of Ellen, and then wondered whether she herself had inherited some of Biddy's sharp tongue. She'd definitely let Alex have it a few times already.

'We should definitely be friends,' Ellen decided for her. 'What're you doing tonight? We could have dinner or something.'

'Oh. I'm busy tonight, I'm afraid.' Connie looked away slightly, not wanting to give Ellen any chance to gossip that she had a date with Alex – especially since Ellen had confessed her crush on him. 'Maybe tomorrow?' She wasn't really over-keen on becoming friends, but she told herself to give Ellen a chance. People could be awkward at first and turn out to be really nice – in fact, Connie herself had probably been awkward with more people than she could remember when first getting to know them. More than one person, including Alex, had described her as cold and aloof before they had got to know her. She had never intended to be like that, but sometimes shyness came over as being cold.

Ellen's face lit up. 'Oh, I'd love that! Shall we go to the Crown and Feathers? Oh, no, they don't do food. Oh! I know. We could go to Alex's new pub. What do you think? I can drive.' She looked excited.

'Oh, well... sure, if you want.' Connie didn't want to tell Ellen she was going there tonight to have dinner with Alex. 'But I'm just as happy to go to the local. Then neither of us has to drive.'

'Oh, I don't mind!' Ellen trilled. 'I'll pick you up. Seven? We'll have a girls' night out! It'll be fun.'

'Okay. Sounds great,' Connie acquiesced, not being able to think of a good reason not to go.

'Perfect! Okay, I'll see you then. Duty calls!' Ellen leaned in unexpectedly and kissed Connie on the cheek.

'The fast-paced world of greeting cards never stops, huh?'

'What? Oh, right. Yes!' Ellen rolled her eyes. 'I'm so glad we're going to be friends!' she laughed, and waved as she walked out.

Connie watched her leave. Esther would be pleased: now Connie had returned to Magpie Cove, her mum was always telling Connie to make friends in the village. Ellen was a bit of a character, but it was a start.

17

'We're the first ones to try this out, so I hope it works.' Alex sounded a little nervous as he lit the coals in the cast iron brazier. 'Here, take a seat.' He stood up as the coals started to flicker red, one by one, a few firelighters helping them catch.

'I don't know what to say. This is so... lovely!' Connie was truly taken aback as she sat down on the quilted seat inside the gorgeous little wooden summer house that Alex had built in the garden adjacent to the pub. Like the main pub garden, it overlooked the sea, but sat alone in a secluded area surrounded by trees behind, and past a gate with a 'Private – No Entry' sign on it.

The summer house had two wooden doors that, when open, made convenient privacy screens on both sides of the seating area, and when closed, protected the inside. As well as the cushioned bench where Connie sat, there were two wicker easy chairs set out next to a glass-topped wicker table on the grass. Inside the summer house a small glass-fronted wine fridge sat next to a couple of shelves which held wine and champagne glasses, and a cool box lay under a small counter.

'Not bad, eh? I had some wood left after we'd done all the work on the pub, so I thought this'd be a nice extra space people could hire out for the evening or whatever. This is its maiden voyage, though.' He grinned shyly at her. 'Glad you like it.'

'I love it!' Connie gazed up at the fairy lights which adorned the roof and the doorframe. 'This is going to be really popular when you let people book it. It's very romantic'

'As promised.' He looked pleased. 'Now for the champagne.'

'Champagne, too? You're really going all out. I'm impressed.' Connie accepted the crystal flute, feeling slightly awkward. She berated herself: Alex was a nice guy, and pretty easy on the eye. There was no need to feel nervous: it wasn't like she'd never had a date before. Yet her stomach was doing flips and she felt like she was sweating. *Attractive.*

'Of course. Brought my A game. Cheers.' He held her gaze as they both sipped the champagne. Neither of them spoke for a few moments, and the heat grew between them as neither looked away. Connie felt pleasurably trapped by Alex's look, as if he was thirstily taking her in. It was a nice feeling, not a threatening one: she knew that he wanted her, and she realised she wanted him too.

There had always been a certain battle of wills between them, but it wasn't a bad thing. Now, it felt more like an enjoyable tension, when, before, he'd irritated the hell out of her. She was aware that some relationships could be like this – a kind of sexy, combative vibe – but she'd never experienced it herself before now. No one had ever taken her to the top of a Cornish cliff and plied her with champagne. It was a lot to take in.

Connie cleared her throat and put her glass down on the table.

'So...' she trailed off, and Alex caught her eye.

'So,' he agreed, nodding seriously. It made her laugh, and the tension was broken.

'No coastal erosion on this side, then? Or could I die in a land-slide at any minute?' Connie took another sip of her champagne, smirking playfully.

'I think we're safe.' Alex narrowed his eyes at the edge of the cliff. 'If we're still sitting here in fifty years, maybe not. And, may I just say, kudos on mentioning coastal erosion on a first date. Winning.'

'Shut up! It's a valid concern,' she giggled. 'I'm nothing if not the perfect romantic.'

'Clearly.' Alex sipped his champagne and gazed out at the setting sun, which glowed over the Cornish sea like an orange torch. 'Luckily, the view makes up for your terrible first-date technique. I never get over the sunsets here, and I've lived here all my life.'

'I know. It's stunning,' Connie breathed, feeling the champagne work its magic: her nervousness was ebbing away, and she started to relax. *This is a beautiful moment on a beautiful evening. Just enjoy it*, she told herself. 'And this is a really lovely date. Thanks for bringing me here.' She looked up, shyly, this time, and met his smile.

'You're very welcome, Connie,' he said, softly, and leaned in for a kiss.

It was only a brief brush of his lips, but it was electric. Even before their lips had met, Connie could feel the energy of Alex, as if he was surrounded by some kind of charged cloud of masculinity that switched on something primal and feminine in her. She closed her eyes and gave herself up to the kiss, receiving his lips softly. He smelled of a subtle, woody aftershave, though perhaps it was the smell of the newly varnished summerhouse too.

He sat back, leaning away; Connie opened her eyes. She wanted more of those kisses, but she was willing to wait.

'Hungry?' he asked, and indicated the cool box. 'I've got some dinner in there for us. Crab salad, fresh rolls, strawberries and cream for after.'

'Oh, that sounds amazing,' Connie turned to watch him open the cool box and start extracting containers and what presumably was the bread, wrapped in a clean cloth, onto the small workspace. 'You've really thought of everything.'

'Well, I tried to. Only the best for Connie Christie,' he said, with a grin.

'I'm honoured.'

'I'm serious.' He set a plate of gold and pink crab mixed in a salad of lettuce, baby tomatoes and avocado in front of her and handed her a knife and fork. 'I've liked you for a long time. Really liked you. D'you know that?'

She didn't know what to say.

'How long?' She felt herself blushing.

'I told you this already. Since we were teenagers.' He placed his own plate on the table and sat down opposite her. 'I always thought you were the prettiest girl in the village. I never knew what to say to you, though. I was really shy when I was younger. And you seemed super popular, but also... sort of aloof. Not for the likes of me.'

Connie snorted.

'I was not popular at all! Where did you get that idea?'

'Well, I always used to hear that you'd been on a date with this guy or another. Even my brother wanted to ask you out, but Trevor said he wasn't allowed.'

'Your brother? What, Tim?' Connie asked in amazement. 'Trevor said he couldn't go out with me? Tim fancied me?'

'Yeah. Your brother Trevor told him if he so much as looked at you, he'd break his arm or something.' Alex shrugged. 'I remember, 'cos I was there, and I really wanted to ask you out too but that kind of put me off. Then after that I decided you were too hoity-toity and told my mum not to set us up. In self-defence, though. You weren't hoity-toity, it was just me being insecure.'

Connie frowned. 'Wow. I had no idea. My brothers could be protective, I guess. And those dates you thought I was on were basically my mother's attempts to marry me off in my teens. She'd arrange these casual drop-ins to all her friends in the village who had sons roughly my age. She'd say, *We'll just stop for a cuppa at Mrs So-and-So's, shall we?* and then when we got there, she'd disappear into the kitchen with the mother and I'd get shut in the living room with some boy or another with them outside the door, waiting for us to fall in love. I hated it.'

Alex laughed. 'Wow. That's hardcore matchmaking. Your mum wanted to marry you off pretty young, even by Cornish standards.'

'I think because she got married young, she thought it was normal,' Connie shrugged.

'Well, I'd have married you.' Alex sounded shy. 'But I was convinced you'd break my heart. I told my mum on no account to set us up, remember?'

'I do remember you saying that, yes.'

Connie blushed again. They both ate in silence for a few moments, then she changed the subject, awkwardly. 'This crab is great.'

'Fresh today,' Alex commented. There was another silence. It wasn't uncomfortable; they were both feeling each other out, learning how to be in each other's company in this new, more romantic way.

'How is your brother?' Connie reached for the bread and spread it with some of the softened salted butter Alex had added to the table in a dish.

'Tiny? He's fine. Married, kids. Works at the farm with Dad; he'll take it over in a few years when Dad finally retires. Mum's been at him for a year or two to step aside, so it won't be much longer now. When she gets a bee in her bonnet about something, she always gets her way.'

'And your younger brother? I can't remember his name.' Connie chewed the buttered bread. 'Goodness, this bread is amazing.'

'From Maude's. Richard, yeah. He's away at agricultural college.' Alex tore a corner off the tiger loaf.

'You didn't want to work at the farm too?' Connie sat back and let her gaze wander over Alex's powerful frame. Finally, she had an opportunity to look at him without pretending she wasn't or having to look away at any minute.

This evening, he'd dressed in a cream cable knit jumper and dark jeans; his tan stood out against the wool and, rather than disguise his wide shoulders and thick arms, the jumper only seemed to accentuate them. He'd had his hair cut, she thought, as it looked neater than before, but there was still a slightly unruly nature to it. Now and again, he reached up to push his fringe away from his eyes.

Connie quietly took in a deep breath and let it out slowly, feeling that same slow desire creep over her again. Yes, Alex Gordon was – objectively and quantifiably – hot. But it was his kindness that made Connie feel she could trust him enough to open herself up to him.

'I did, for a few years. But I wanted something of my own, you know? Tim'll get the dairy in a year or so, and Rich'll probably end up going elsewhere to farm. Anyway, a year or so ago, my grandma died and Mum and Dad sold her place. They gave me a lump sum so that I could buy the pub and do it up. I was lucky to have that. You know. Not everyone gets that kind of opportunity.'

'You're lucky to have your family around you like that,' Connie reflected. 'I mean, I spent years trying to get away. Not from them, but from the village. And then my dad died and Trevor and Kevin both left with the Navy, and now it's just me and mum and Uncle Bill, and neither of them're getting any younger.'

'That must've been hard, to lose your dad.' Alex reached for her hand over the table. 'I'm so sorry. I remember him. He was a good bloke.'

'He was,' Connie remembered. 'Anyway, let's not talk about that.' She shivered.

'You're cold? Hang on, there's a blanket here somewhere.' Alex got up, opened a wooden compartment under the cushioned bench and pulled out a thick baby blue wool blanket. 'Come on. You've finished your dinner?'

Connie smiled. 'Stuffed. I'll have to give it half an hour before I can manage any strawberries.'

'Okay. Well, come and get under the blanket for a while and warm up, then.' He patted the cushion next to him. 'Don't be shy.'

'All right.' Connie sat next to him on the bench and Alex arranged the blanket around them both.

'Chilly, these Cornish summer evenings,' he murmured; it was hardly cold, but there was a cool breeze coming in off the sea and Connie was wearing a thin summer dress.

'They can be,' Connie replied in a low voice. She was very aware of Alex's body next to hers. She wanted him; she wanted to kiss him and run her hands over his muscular chest. She wanted to feel that electricity again.

He leaned towards her, tucking the blanket in around her shoulders.

'How's that?' he asked, huskily. His lips were very close to hers: if she just moved a little closer to him, they would touch. She met his gaze.

'Good,' she breathed. His eyes were such a dark brown, she couldn't see his pupils in the dim evening light. The sun was almost set, and the firelight played on his skin. She wanted to inhale him, to taste him and savour him on her tongue.

'Good,' he repeated, holding back, taking his time. Impatiently, letting her instincts take over, Connie wrapped her arms around his neck and drew him to her.

'I like you too, Alex,' she murmured, kissing the corner of his mouth softly. He let out a deep, shuddering breath. His hands found her waist and travelled up her back, pulling her closer to him.

As the sun finally set over the sea, darkness took over, and Alex kissed her. It began softly, then grew deeper and more full of urgent longing.

The leaping fire in the brazier and the twinkling fairy lights played on their faces as the kiss deepened; Connie was aware of nothing apart from Alex and his touch. Slowly, the night got darker, and, as the stars started to dot the Cornish sky, Connie pursued the lines of his body with her fingers. There was a sweetness in him, in his touch and in his kisses, that she'd never known before. The gruff Alex Gordon she knew in the outside world was nothing like this man, whose touch made her glow with its adoration.

She lost track of time, and, finally, fell asleep with her head on his chest, the blanket over them both, and the stars over them both like guardians.

18

'Red or white? My treat.' Ellen fidgeted as they stood at the bar, waiting to be served. She had a kind of nervous quality to her, Connie realised, and she always seemed to be moving: drumming her fingers on the bar, adjusting her handbag strap, humming distractedly. Esther would have called her a *fiddle-fingers* or a *flibbertigibbet* if she'd been there. Connie suppressed a smile at the thought.

'White would be nice. It's a bit hot for red.' Connie lifted her hair off her neck and twisted it into a rough bun with a hairband from her wrist. The wide glass doors to the pub garden were open and a couple of ceiling fans rotated lazily above, but it was a hot night again. She could feel a trickle of sweat between her shoulders, and was thankful she'd chosen her lightest sundress to wear for the evening.

She hadn't yet mentioned to Ellen that she'd just been at the pub the night before with Alex, and had in fact fallen asleep in his arms under the stars. They'd woken up in the middle of the night, stiff and chilly, and Alex had driven her home in his Land Rover, along the empty, winding lanes. They hadn't talked much, and Connie had half-drowsed for the whole journey, half in dream as the soft roads of her childhood unfurled under them.

He'd kissed her again before she got out of the car and watched until she let herself in, although they must have been the only ones up at that hour. Magpie Cove had a magic feeling to it last night, under a full moon and with the stars patterning the inky blue-black sky like diamonds. Connie couldn't say for sure whether it was always like that in the wee small hours, or whether there was some kind of romantic sheen to her perception, because of her date with Alex.

She hadn't heard from him since, which was fine – it hadn't exactly been long, and they were both busy. Yet, the thought of possibly seeing him again tonight sent a delicious chill of anticipation up her spine.

'I didn't expect to see you.' As if she'd summoned him with her thoughts, Alex's voice rumbled softly in her ear, and Connie felt his hand in the small of her back.

'Oh. Hi.' She felt herself blushing and willed it to stop. It felt like everyone in the pub was staring at them, and everyone must know that they'd kissed. Yet, looking around, nobody was watching them except Ellen, whose expression showed plainly that she understood what Alex's close proximity to Connie, and his murmured tone, meant.

'Evening, Ellen.' Alex took a step away from Connie so that he was standing in the neutral space between them. 'Good to see you.'

'Ellen asked me up here for a drink,' Connie explained brightly. 'We thought we'd come and support the pub, now you're open for business.'

'Ah, I see.' Alex smiled genially at Ellen. 'And you're very welcome, of course. Let me find you a table outside.' He picked up a tray from the side of the bar and placed their bottle of Sauvignon Blanc and two glasses on it, carrying it out into the garden.

'Well, isn't that nice?' Ellen muttered, following Alex outside.

She sat down in the chair that Alex pulled out for her and let him pour wine into both glasses. The bottle looked perfectly chilled, the golden liquid prompting a dew on the outside of the glass as soon as it was poured.

'I'll leave you to it, then.' Alex's eyes lingered on Connie's. She couldn't help returning his gaze – the air crackled between them with unspoken desire. Alex's eyes were so dark and soft, and she could feel herself being drawn into them. She remembered his soft touch on her skin, his urgent kisses, and felt her temperature rise in a way that was nothing to do with the hot summer night. 'See you later, maybe, Connie,' he added in a low voice.

'Sure. See you later.' She cleared her throat from the pent-up longing that seemed to have settled there, but even so, it came out croakily. She took a sip of wine to cover her awkwardness, and watched him out of the corner of her eye and he gave her a seductive grin and walked back into the pub.

'Well, if he'd stayed much longer, I think I would've had to hose you both down!' Ellen exclaimed, putting her wine glass back on the glass-topped rattan table that sat between them. She was grinning, but Connie thought she detected a sad look in Ellen's eyes for a brief moment. 'So. Tell me everything.'

'About what?' Connie feigned innocence, but Ellen just laughed.

'Oh, you're a sly miss, you are! You and Alex Gordon have clearly got something going on. I wondered about it at the party, and I was right! See, I've got a sixth sense about these things.' She sat back in her wicker armchair and regarded Connie with an unreadable look. 'Come on. Spill it.'

'It's really nothing,' she tried, but Ellen shook her head vehemently.

'No way, Connie Christie! You're not going to fob me off. I saw the way he looked at you just now. You lucky mare.'

'I'm sorry, I know you like him.' Connie frowned. 'I... he asked me out. We went on a date last night.'

'Well, yes, of course I like him. Every single woman around here likes Alex Gordon. Some that aren't single, too,' Ellen added. 'Doesn't mean you should feel guilty about going out with him. He'd never look at me the way he just looked at you. It's that perfect hair and big blue eyes you've got. Bet you get men following you home every night.' Ellen sounded wistful.

Connie gave Ellen a sharp look. Was that some kind of hint that Ellen knew something about her stalker – about what had happened the other day? The 'I'M WATCHING YOU' scratched on the back door of the museum?

'It's not something nice, being followed,' Connie replied, shortly. 'No, it doesn't happen every night. But yes, it has happened, and it's scary. I'd rather not have my hair and eyes if that's what causes it, but I don't think it's even that. Just some men think it's their right to do things like that to women, and they don't know how terrifying it is.'

Connie took a long gulp of wine to steady her nerves. Ellen's comment had riled her a little, and the evening's mood had suddenly shifted from something pleasant to something quite different.

'Haven't you seen the posters around the village? The ones that the teenagers have put up? No one should get followed home, or catcalled, or made to feel uncomfortable in any way,' Connie continued.

'Oh, gosh, I didn't mean it like that. I'm sorry.' Ellen reached across the table and clasped Connie's hand in hers. 'I know what that's like, anyway. Happened to me once or twice when I was younger. Fortunately, I had my sister to look after me.' A shadow passed over her face. 'I didn't mean it badly, like. I was just being a bit of a jealous mare. But you'd be good together, you and Alex, I can see that.' Ellen squeezed Connie's hand and let it go. 'He had his heart broken before, I think. Probably ready for someone to come along and mend it now.'

'Ah, well, I don't know about that. It's very early days.' Connie looked away, embarrassed. She'd found herself thinking about Alex a lot, and she would have been lying if she said she hadn't thought about where it might lead, especially after last night. But she had to remain realistic: they'd had one date, and while it had been amazing, that was all it was so far.

'See where it goes.' Ellen shrugged. 'Worst case, you have a bloody good time with Magpie Cove's most eligible bachelor for a bit. Top-up?' She brandished the bottle at Connie, who laughed.

'Go on then.' She held out her glass for a refill. Ellen had seemed like a bit of an odd duck, but Connie was starting to like her.

Connie's phone was on the table between them, and the screen lit up. She leaned over and picked it up.

'Someone wants you,' Ellen observed. Connie opened the text. It was from Georgia, the manager at her old theatre in Plymouth.

Hi, Connie, hope all's well in the back of beyond? Just wanted to let you know that we've received some new funding and planning to reopen in September for a new season. Would love to have you back, if you're interested? Starting prep for Uncle Vanya, *then two more shows next year. Let me know, Georgia xx*

'What is it?' Ellen leaned in, curiously.

'Oh. My old manager at the theatre. They're reopening.' Connie re-read the text. 'Wow. That's a surprise.' She sat back and thought about going back to the theatre again. She couldn't deny that she'd missed it.

'The theatre?' Ellen sipped her wine. 'Why'd you leave in the first place? Sounds like a fun job. I'd do anything to get out of Magpie Cove.'

'They lost their funding. I'm surprised they managed to get anything new, it's not a great time for theatres right now.' Connie took a drink, playing with her wine glass stem. 'But I promised Mum, and I've spent all this effort relaunching the museum and the tours. I dunno, it seems a shame to leave it just when it's got started.'

'Well, I'd go if I could. Wouldn't give this place a backwards glance,' Ellen scoffed. Connie was just about to ask her why she apparently hated the village so much – and what was holding her back if she wanted to go – when there was the sound of breaking glass and a woman's shout of surprise. Connie looked around but couldn't see anything at first, though the noise seemed to have come from the back of the garden, near the cliff edge.

'What was that?' Connie frowned.

'I don't know,' Ellen replied, though she had a strangely watchful look.

Connie got up and wandered to the edge of the garden; a small crowd was forming there. One of the waiters had gone running inside and came back with Alex, who strode swiftly to the fence at the edge of the garden.

'All right, nothing to see. Just a bit of rock fall,' he called out, facing Connie and the few other men and women who'd come over to see what was happening. A woman sitting at the table near the edge of the garden had fallen off her chair, which was the noise Connie had heard. What she hadn't realised was that the woman had been thrown off her balance by the ground shifting suddenly underneath her. Even though the edge of the cliff face was fenced off, one of the trees in their sizeable pots Alex had placed at the edge had disappeared. Connie tried to peer over the edge, but he held her back.

'Don't stand too close to the edge,' he warned, his hands wrapping instinctively around her waist.

'Alex, you've got to get these people inside.' Connie could just see the palm tree at the bottom of the cliffs, its huge terracotta pot broken into shards. 'It's dangerous.'

'It was just the edge,' he argued, though he looked shaken. 'I've had the survey done. It shouldn't go any further.'

'Alex. It's a cliff. You know the coast's dangerous around here.' Connie twisted around in his grip and faced him. 'Come on. Get these people inside for tonight, then call out the surveyor tomorrow. You don't want to risk anything worse happening.'

'All right, all right,' he grunted, beckoning to two of his waiters. 'Guys, can you get everyone inside, please? Give them a free round of drinks to persuade them. Say we've got some... errr... structural problems we just have to sort out for now.'

'I think that's the right thing to do,' Connie approved. 'I'll give you a hand getting everyone moved.' She looked back at her table where Ellen had been, but her friend had disappeared. 'Ellen must be inside already.'

Yet it was more than an hour later – after she'd helped Alex fence off the cliff edge with warning tape and gone back inside – that Connie realised Ellen wasn't inside the pub, and had left without saying goodbye.

19

Connie held a small bouquet of roses to her chest, waiting by the rusted iron gate to the only cemetery in Magpie Cove.

The church, a small stone chapel dating from the 1600s, sat behind her: ancient yew trees surrounded it, and white roses in full bloom twisted around the church door and up its walls. The local vicar, Mary, had changed things in the time Connie had been away from the village; Esther told her that the new vicar – *a woman!* – did much better services than old Father Landman, who had christened Connie and her brothers and mumbled through his services once a week to a failing congregation. In fact, Connie had been to church with her mum a couple of times since she'd been back and Esther was right – the sermons were thought-provoking, the songs were better, and word had clearly got around, because the chapel had been more or less full every time.

However, today, Connie wasn't here for a service.

'Oh, you weren't waiting long, were you?' Ellen Robb puffed her way up the path towards the gate, waving at Connie. 'Lovely day for it.' She gestured at the sapphire blue sky above. There was a light breeze coming off the sea, and since the church sat on the hill, you could look across the Cove and out to sea.

'Yes, it is.' Connie gazed around her. 'It's a pretty goth thing to invite people to a cemetery for fun, you know,' she teased Ellen.

Ellen had texted her a couple of days after their drink at the pub, apologising for her sudden disappearance, and suggesting that they meet at the church to lay flowers on their respective great-great-grandmother's graves.

Think of it like we're putting an end to it, Ellen had texted. *All that arguing. We can be friends now and heal those old wounds between Biddy and Rosemary.*

It was a strange thing to be doing on a Wednesday morning, but Connie was getting used to the idea that Ellen saw life a little differently to the norm. And, anyway, it was a good idea. There was something nicely symbolic in Ellen's idea that they would each lay flowers on the other's ancestor's grave.

'Look, I'm sorry I disappeared, the other night.' Ellen looked uncomfortable. 'Bit of family difficulty. I had to go straight away, and you were busy with Alex in the garden. Sorry.'

'That's okay. I was just concerned you were all right.' Connie was relieved there was an explanation for Ellen's sudden absence. 'What was the family difficulty?'

'Oh, you know,' Ellen said, vaguely. 'My sister Junie's not so good at the moment.'

'Oh! I hope she's all right.'

Ellen made a dismissive gesture. 'Oh, yeah. Bit of rest is all she needed.'

'I know what it's like, though. Uncle Bill's really not well, and he refuses to go to the doctor. And Mum isn't as sharp as she was. Not that she'd admit it,' Connie confessed.

'Don't get old, I s'pose.' Ellen shrugged. 'Shall we?' She gestured at the stones that dotted the tussocky green turf. 'This way, I think.'

Like many of them, Biddy Christie's grey gravestone was spotted white with age.

HERE LIES BIDDY CHRISTIE
1890–1941
OLD MAID
A GOOD WOMAN

Ellen read the words on the gravestone aloud.

'Blimey. I hope they don't put that on mine,' she added.

'What?' Connie watched as Ellen knelt in front of Biddy's grave. Someone – Esther, Connie supposed – had put one of those graveside vases with the separate holes at the top for flowers on the flat part of the stone. Ellen threaded the pink carnations she'd brought with her into the holes.

'Old Maid,' Ellen replied. 'Bloody judgemental.'

'Well, that was a thing in those days. I don't think they put that on graves anymore,' Connie smiled.

Ellen stood up. 'Feel like we should say something. How about I say something to Biddy and you say something to Rosemary?'

'That sounds fair,' Connie replied.

'Right. Err...' Ellen thought for a moment, and then closed her eyes. 'Biddy Christie, I hope you found rest in the afterlife with the angels and what have you. I hope that you can forgive my great-great-grandmother Rosemary Connor for being a right mare sometimes. She said you were a witch and you weren't – well, even if you were, it was none of her business, probably. And I'm sorry she stole your boyfriend Sam, though I think they were quite happy in the end. Rest in peace, Biddy.'

Ellen opened her eyes and self-consciously tapped the top of Biddy's gravestone.

'Was that all right?'

'It was surprisingly moving, actually. Thank you. This was a really nice idea, you know.'

'Thanks.' Ellen glowed with pride. 'I'm glad you came. I thought you might think I was being a bit mad.'

'Well, I did, but then I realised you were right,' Connie grinned. 'Right. Let's go and do Rosemary now, shall we?'

Ellen led the way to the other side of the small cemetery.

'Here she is,' she said, standing next to a larger gravestone that read:

ROSEMARY ROBB, NEE CONNOR
1887–1968
BELOVED WIFE AND MOTHER
Be faithful unto death, and I will give you the crown of life –
Ephesians 2:10

'D'you think it was on purpose, putting them on opposite sides of the graveyard?' Connie looked over to Biddy's grave.

'Definitely. The Christies all get buried on that side, we get buried on this one. Always been that way. Even the church knew there was grudges going back years.'

'I wonder who started it. You know, in the beginning.' Connie unwrapped her roses and placed them in the vase recess that was helpfully cut into the gravestone. Unlike Biddy's, which looked like the original stone, this one had clearly been replaced more recently, as it was in white marble with cleanly etched black letters.

'Dunno.' Ellen shook her head. 'But likely it wasn't Biddy and Rosemary. Just playing out something bigger than them.' She looked thoughtful, but didn't say any more.

'Hmm.' Connie stood up and wondered what to say. She gazed at the horizon, watching seagulls drift on the thermals above the cove.

'Rosemary, I can't say exactly what Biddy would have wanted to say to you, because I don't know. But I know that neither of you were bad people. Like Ellen says, you were probably reacting to some kind of family antagonism that went back generations before you. Biddy was in love with Sam, but I believe that he loved you – he married you and I know you had a happy family life together. I wonder whether, when you started rumours about Biddy being a witch, you were actually nervous about what people thought of you, learning to be an apothecary at a time when it was unusual for women to have any education.'

Connie paused, watching the seagulls, thinking about Biddy. How Biddy had probably felt as persecuted as she had, as a teenager. How, in some ways, their experiences were alike.

'Rosemary, I want you to know that I forgive you on behalf of the Christie family. I want you to know that I respect your knowledge and education, and that you made a good life in hard times. Perhaps, wherever you are now, you and Biddy can be friends.'

Connie bowed her head.

'That was much better than mine.' Ellen sniffed. 'Feel like I should go back and say more to old Biddy now.'

'No, it was fine.' Connie jammed her hands in her pockets and looked around. 'So, what now?'

'Dunno. Maybe we should sing a song,' Ellen suggested, dubiously.

'No, I think we're done.' Connie took in a deep breath. 'We've let go of the past. It feels good, don't you think?'

Ellen considered it for a minute, then smiled too.

'I think so. And it feels good being your friend.' She reached out, awkwardly, and squeezed Connie's shoulder. 'Are we friends now?'

Connie smiled. 'I guess so.'

After they'd had a wander around the old churchyard, Ellen had left, saying that she had things to do at home. Connie was due to open up the museum, but she lingered a while, enjoying the sun as she sat with her back against one of the old graves. Despite the fact that it was a graveyard, it was a lovely spot, completely quiet apart from the sound of birdsong and the peaceful crash of the surf below.

She closed her eyes, listening to the birds and the waves, and let herself enjoy the moment. The sunlight was bright on her face. Everything was calm.

She jumped as a shadow crossed over the sun, and the sound of someone walking past.

She opened her eyes. She really thought that she'd heard footsteps, but there was no one there.

A shiver ran up her spine. Standing up, Connie scanned the graveyard, but there was no sign of anyone.

You're just being silly, she told herself. *It could have been anything: a bird, a cloud over the sun. The wind on the grass, sounding like someone walking past.*

Yet, suddenly, Connie didn't feel peaceful anymore. She picked up her bag and made her way out of the graveyard, looking over her shoulder. It was time to go: she needed to get to work anyway.

The sun shone and the birds sang as before: nothing was different. *You're just imagining it,* Connie repeated, in her head. *There's no one else here.*

Yet, as she walked through the iron gate, Connie heard a low laugh from the other side of the graveyard, and a voice call out:

'I'm watching you, Connie. From beyond the graaaaave.'

Without thinking, Connie's temper snapped.

'Hazel, is that you?' she cried out, making her way across the graveyard. 'Come here and say that. Show yourself!'

Connie rounded the edge of the church building, but still there was no one there. She raced around to the other side. Nobody to be seen.

'Coward!' Connie shouted into the morning air. A curlew squawked in the air, but otherwise there was silence. 'If it's you, Hazel, leave me alone! I'm not scared of you!' she cried out again, but there was no reply.

Furious, Connie made her way back to the high street. She had absolutely had enough of this now and was going to put a stop to it, once and for all.

20

'Don't worry. It's going to be great! You sold all the tickets.' Lila Bridges from the café gave Connie a spur-of-the-moment hug. 'This is so great, Connie! I'm so excited. I haven't been to the cinema in ages.'

'Well, it's not really a cinema,' Connie demurred. 'More of a bed sheet and a projector. But, yeah. I'm looking forward to it, as long as everything works.'

'It will. And the food and drink's all sorted.'

'Thank you so much for helping me out with that, Lila. It's brilliant.' Connie eyed the golden-yellow quiches speckled with flecks of red pepper and green spinach, beautiful glazed vegetable tarts cut into slices and plates of cheese and crackers. Lila had added bowls of crisps, wine, beer and soft drinks, and an array of delicious-looking cakes.

'No trouble. It's fun to cater community events,' Lila grinned. 'The only problem might be stopping Oliver from eating everything before anyone gets here. Hey! Hands off!' Lila called out to a tall, blond man who was hovering by the food table. He was immaculately dressed in what looked like a silky designer jet black T-shirt and – rather unseasonably for the warm weather – a black-and-grey kilt.

'Oh, excuse me, but I think you'll find I made these madeleines – oh, *and* the macarons. So I'm perfectly at liberty to try one, Miss Bridges.' He snapped his fingers at her and sashayed over to Connie. 'I don't think we've actually met, have we? I'm Oliver Kay. I run a private catering business. We're in the premises that used to be the old café at the end of the street.'

'Oh, hi! Yes. The café that was never open.' Connie shook Oliver's hand. 'I'm Connie Christie. I just took over the museum from my uncle Bill.'

'Oh, bless Bill. How is he?' Oliver bit into a bright pink macaron. 'He's such a dear.'

'He's all right, thanks. My mum's got him on a healthy eating regime now, though we can't get him to give up his pipe. I did invite him tonight but he said it wasn't his cup of tea. And he had a date anyway.' Connie rolled her eyes.

'Oooh, he's a ladykiller, that one!' Oliver grinned. 'Hey. *I* wouldn't miss a Katharine Hepburn movie showing for all the tea in China. I'm so excited. *And* in a darling little Cornish museum too. Talk about atmosphere! You know, we held an eightieth birthday party here for one of the ladies in the village a couple of years back. It was lovely then, but you've made such a lot of improvements! Really cleaned the place up. And I love your new exhibits.'

'Oh, thanks so much. I just had the time and energy to do it, that's all. Uncle Bill was too tired to be up ladders, cleaning the skylights and repainting walls.'

'Well, it looks fab, anyway,' Oliver congratulated her. 'Look, when you're not museum-ing, you should come out for a drink with me and Lila. There's that new pub up on Morven Head, isn't there? I've heard it's nice. Also that the new owner's a bit of a dish.' He gave Connie an exaggerated wink.

'Oh, Connie knows all about Alex Gordon.' Lila joined them, drinking from a bottle of sparkling water. 'You're too late, Oli. She's claimed Magpie Cove's most eligible bachelor already.'

'Oh, really?' Oliver's eyes widened. 'Tell me everything. I want all the gory details.'

'Well, maybe later,' Connie laughed as the attendees started to arrive. 'I've got to go and check tickets for now.'

'All right, but don't think I've forgotten about you, because I haven't.' Oliver wagged his finger at her theatrically.

'Ladies and gentlemen, thank you so much for joining us tonight for what I hope might become a semi-regular event.' Connie stood at the front of the museum and addressed the hall. She'd pushed many of the cabinets back and arranged a few rows of chairs in front of the bed sheet she'd borrowed from her mum for the evening, which she'd securely pegged out straight on two clothing lines strung ingeniously between the two steel girders that held the mezzanine up.

She'd been a little freaked out after thinking someone was watching her at the graveyard, but organising the film night over the past couple of weeks had given her the distraction she'd needed to put it into perspective. The churchyard up on the hill above Magpie Cove was old, and while it was a beautiful spot, it was still a graveyard. Even if you weren't inclined to believe in ghosts, graveyards could be spooky places, and Connie had rationalised that there probably *had* been someone else there when she had.

Whoever it was up there that day had either *been playing silly beggars*, as Esther liked to say, and had decided to give Connie a bit of a scare. Though she'd shouted out Hazel's name, she still didn't quite believe a woman of almost thirty would hang around graveyards and call out insults, but stranger things had happened.

When she'd got home, she'd sent Hazel a message on social media: she was easy enough to find online, with a whole *House Beautiful*-style Instagram account detailing her beautiful home, her two Chihuahuas and various pouty selfies. If Hazel was the one trying to intimidate her, then she was due a note from someone else for a change. Connie had written:

Dear Hazel,

I'm writing this, firstly, to apologise for slamming the museum door in your face the other day. I recognise that this was not a very adult thing to do, and in fact we are both adults now, and not school friends. Not that we were ever very good friends, in my recollection anyway.

However, I thought that I should get in touch and let you know that the reason I might have been quite harsh with you the other day is that since I've been back in Magpie Cove, someone has been leaving me abusive notes. I've also experienced being followed, and some criminal damage at the museum which I have reported to the police.

This harassment mirrors other actions and notes which I received twelve years ago, before leaving Magpie Cove. I believe the abusive notes come from the same person.

Without putting too fine a point on it, I believe that this person might be you. Is it?

I can't prove that it is, but with your history of bullying behaviour and because of the comments you made the other day – that I 'always thought I was better than everyone else, but I'm not and never were' – which is very similar to some of the messages I've received – you can understand my suspicion.

I would like, most of all, for this harassment to stop. I am happy for us to meet and talk, if this is something you would like to do.

If I've got this all wrong, please let me know that too.

Connie

Having sent the message, Connie felt, if not closure, then at least a satisfaction at being firm and open with the person who might have been behind the notes. Once it was gone – and she saw that Hazel had read it – she busied herself sourcing extra chairs for the film night, selling tickets and finding out if you needed permission to screen a film from 1939 in a museum.

'For those of you that don't know me, I'm Connie Christie, and my family have owned the Shipwreck and Smuggling Museum for many years now. Tonight, we're diverging a little from shipwrecks and smuggling, though, as I wanted to take this opportunity to introduce you to my new exhibit, Women of Cornwall.'

Connie surveyed the crowd as she described what was in the new exhibit, and why she'd decided to hold an evening focused on strong women and women's empowerment. Alex hadn't been able to come, as he was at the pub, and Esther was at her knitting circle. Other than that, she recognised Maude from the bakery opposite and Mara Hughes who sometimes worked at the café too. She guessed that many members of the audience were made up of the teen girls' families and some tourists. Indeed, Mara was sitting next to one of the teen girls, Franny. Ellen Robb sat in the front row, beaming.

Connie cleared her throat, feeling nervous.

'Anyway, before we move onto our feature film for this evening, *The Philadelphia Story*, I'm going to hand over to four young women campaigning to make Magpie Cove a better place for us all. Seren, Franny, Lola and Indigo, please come and join me.'

There was some good-natured whooping from the crowd as the teens came to stand next to Connie, who stood aside and let them talk.

After the presentations and the film, everyone milled around the museum, eating Lila's delicious food, having a few drinks and chatting. Connie was pleased to see that some people were taking the opportunity to have a proper look around the museum too.

She was hungrily piling a plate with vegetable quiche and crisps when Ellen nudged her arm.

'Connie! This was so great. Brilliant idea for a fun evening.'

'Oh, thanks, Ellen. Wine?'

'Love one. Thanks.'

Connie poured two glasses of wine and handed one to Ellen.

'I heard that you had a bit of a barny with Hazel Goody a couple of weeks ago, by the way,' Ellen said in a low voice. 'I remember her from school, not that she'd remember me, of course. Right nasty piece of work.'

'Yeah, I did.' Connie looked around anxiously, as if Hazel was going to pop out of the woodwork any minute. 'Haven't seen her since. I half thought she'd come tonight...' she trailed off, not wanting to explain to Ellen why she thought that. At the very least, she'd expected a response, but there had been nothing.

'Not if you'd had a barny, though,' Ellen replied.

'Maybe,' Connie said, doubtfully. 'Anyway, what did you think?'

'Oh, it was brilliant!' Ellen enthused. 'Makes a change to have something to do of an evening, if I'm honest. Most nights I'm at home, watching paint dry.'

'Not much to do in Magpie Cove,' Connie agreed. 'I guess I can tell that by the fact I sold out tickets in two days for a screening of a very old film.'

'Hmm. Well, I'd better go, anyway. I just wanted to say congratulations.' Ellen drained her wine glass and gave Connie a big smile. 'See you soon, though?'

'Sure. Hang around for a bit now, if you want. I think people will be here a while, and we've got wine.'

'Oh, no. That's a lovely idea, but I've got to get home for Junie.'

'Junie?' Connie frowned.

'My sister. She can be a bit... difficult sometimes.'

'Oh, right, I remember. Difficult?'

'Oh, you know. Sister stuff.' Ellen looked evasive. 'Anyway, I'd better go.'

'Fair enough. See you soon, then.' Connie hurried to put her wine glass down on a nearby chair as Ellen tried to hug her awkwardly. ''Bye.'

''Bye, Connie.' Ellen reminded Connie of a little field mouse, scurrying back home. She wondered what Junie was like; it was odd that they'd never met, especially now that she and Ellen had become friends.

'Penny for 'em.' Oliver reappeared at her side. 'Everything okay?' He followed Connie's gaze as Ellen let herself out of the museum.

'No, I'm... it's fine, thanks,' Connie smiled.

'That was great fun, missus! We'll have to have another show-ing. Perhaps a Barbra Streisand film next time. Just a suggestion,' Oliver rambled on.

'All suggestions welcome.'

'Good. Now then, come and meet Mara and Brian before they take Franny home. She was good, wasn't she? Doing her speech. I tell you, I've got high hopes for our future feminists. Anyway, the teens are heading off with their mums and dads now, so Lila and me and Nathan – that's Lila's fella, over there – thought we'd get rid of the last of your customers in a bit and have a lock-in,' he whispered theatrically. 'Sound good?'

Connie looked around her: at the museum, at the people laughing and having a good time.

She'd forgotten the pleasure she took in putting on a good show: the sense of satisfaction at the end when everything had gone to plan. It made her think about the theatre again, and realise how much she missed it.

'Sounds good.'

21

Connie was steering the *Pirate Queen* away from the third cove on her route back home.

It had been a good day: it was the start of the school summer holidays and the boat was at full capacity. There was even a waiting list for the boat tours for the next couple of weeks: word had got out that it was good, and Connie had seen a lot of positive reviews on the local tourist sites. Despite her dislike of performing, she'd actually realised that she enjoyed showing people around the coves, and even got into the spirit of telling some of Uncle Bill's old smuggling tales. Her favourite story was about the Carter family of Prussia Cove, down the coast towards Penzance. She tried to stay as faithful to Uncle Bill's telling of the story as she could, though she knew she couldn't quite rival his soft Cornish burr – coupled with the fact he was an *actual* fisherman, with a huge white beard.

Bear in mind, maid, Uncle Bill would always lean towards her during his story and wag his finger. *Bear in mind that we says smugglin' now like it's a bad thing. An' it was, but everyone was in on it then. Even the magistrates turned a blind eye. Smugglin' was all a lot of Cornish families 'ad, then. They was poor as dirt.*

Connie sometimes wondered whether it was Uncle Bill's stories of ships and battles that had inspired both of her brothers to join the Navy, though she knew it was mostly because there were few jobs to be had in Cornwall, and they'd both wanted to see the world.

Connie had got into the habit of intoning the final line of the story – 'To this day, local legend has it that a tunnel exists from the cove, maybe leading to the remains of a castle inland' – as dramatically as she could. Usually, there was a collective drawing-in of breath from the customers, followed by a raft of questions.

She'd just finished the tale of the Carter brothers when the *Pirate Queen*'s motor cut out completely. She turned the key in the ignition, expecting the motor to sputter back into life, but it was dead.

She turned the key again, looking back at the boat full of tourists who were chatting among themselves, taking pictures and staring out contentedly at the horizon. *Come on, come on*, she willed the engine, but nothing happened.

Oh no.

Connie checked the fuel levels, but they were fine. However, there was a flashing error message on the boat's outboard motor display. Frowning, she looked around for the boat's manual so she could look the code number up, but she couldn't see it anywhere. Dimly, she remembered Uncle Bill borrowing it a week ago so that he could check on some part he had to order for the boat.

Damn.

Smiling at the tourists, Connie turned the ignition again, and came up with nothing.

Okay. Don't panic, she told herself.

Without the motor, she could already see that the strong tide outside this particular cove was starting to push the *Pirate Queen* out into the sea, which was a problem. It was around four o'clock in the afternoon and it had been a balmy summer's day, but on the horizon, Connie could see a rolling wall of purplish-grey cloud. It had been threatening for a few days and was now on its way in. It was the way of the weather when it had been this hot: after a week or so, the pressure would mount up and a storm would break, relieving the thirty-degree heat and the close, airless nights.

Connie liked a good storm as much as the next person, but it wasn't nearly as appealing if you were stranded on a boat with no shelter, and in fear of the choppy tides that the wind would bring.

All right. She'd have to take control, and quickly, otherwise things could go wrong very fast.

'May I have your attention, please?' Connie shouted, clapping her hands. She felt foolish, but there was a procedure that had to be followed in this situation. Uncle Bill had trained her and her brothers since they were kids: in the event of a breakdown, anchor the boat and call for help. At least everyone was already wearing a life jacket: she would never leave the harbour without making sure of that. She also had emergency rations on board and a box of as-yet unused pac-a-macs which it definitely looked like she might need, if the storm came in as fast as she anticipated.

'It seems that we're experiencing some mechanical difficulties, so I'm going to call for help from the coastguard. There's nothing to worry about, but we may be stuck here for a while, I'm afraid,' Connie announced as brightly as she could. 'I'm going to ask this gentleman here to help me pass you all a mac, in case the weather changes, and I've got water and drinks still on board as well as snacks, so we'll open those up. There is a bathroom, in the galley, for those that need it. All right?'

Her customers exchanged a few glances, but seemed more or less agreeable. Connie gave her most winning smile to one of the dads on board and showed him where the cool box and the pac-a-macs were; thankfully, he was happy to help and started handing everything out calmly.

Having checked the tourists were relatively all right, Connie was aware that she had to anchor the boat quickly; without the engine, they would drift fast, which was bad. Unfortunately, they were in deeper water than she'd have liked, and she hoped her anchor would still do the job. Anchoring in deep water could be an issue if you couldn't stop the boat moving, or if you didn't have a long enough rode, the twisted nylon line and chain that attached to the anchor.

She had a spare anchor on board, but her usual claw anchor should do the job, as long as the sea bed wasn't too rocky where they were.

Carefully, using the mechanical windlass Uncle Bill had fitted some years ago, Connie lowered the anchor off the bow of the *Pirate Queen*. Usually, when you anchored up, you dropped anchor and then reversed the boat, letting the chain pull out to the right length to keep the boat firmly tethered. Without her motor, she had to drop anchor and hope that the wind and the tide would pull the boat against the anchor to keep it steady.

Tying off her ropes and having stopped the chain at what she hoped was the right length, she looked back at her customers, waiting to feel the resistance of the *Pirate Queen* against the taut chain. Thankfully, she felt it after a few moments, and looked at the shore to gauge where they were. Distantly, she could see Alex's pub up on Morven Head, and wished she was there, sipping a glass of white wine. She hadn't seen him for a few days and she missed him.

Still, there wasn't time for thinking about that now. Connie reached into her pocket, found her phone and called the coastguard.

22

'Fuel line's been messed with,' Uncle Bill grunted from under the *Pirate Queen*'s motor. 'Clamps 're missin,' he tutted, standing up and wiping his hands on a rag. 'I take it you never took 'em off, maid?'

'No, of course not.' Connie pulled the cord of her rain mac hood tight around her face: it was pouring with rain now, and the last of the tourists were finally off the boat. She'd promised to give them all a refund: it was the least she could do, considering they'd had to sit on the boat for two hours in the rain before the coastguard appeared and towed them back to Magpie Cove. 'Could they just come off naturally? On their own?'

'Nah. Someone took 'em off on purpose.' Uncle Bill sucked his teeth. 'I never known it 'appen jus on its own, like.'

'But why would anyone do that?' Connie asked, in amazement.

Uncle Bill shook his head. 'Playin' silly beggars.'

'Mind you, you'd 'ave ter know what you were doin'. Ye caint do it by accident. 'Ave ter know yer way around motors a bit,' Constable Chalmers interjected, peering at Uncle Bill under the boat. Connie had found him on the harbour with Uncle Bill as the coastguard had finally towed the *Pirate Queen* into shore.

'Oh, my goodness.' Connie stared at the motor. 'But the motor lost power when we'd already been out for a couple of hours. No one on the boat could have done it. I was with them the whole time.'

'Naw. Ye can remove the clamps wot holds the fuel line onto the fuel tank. Then it'd probably have worked itself loose wi' the movement of the boat.' Uncle Bill sighed. 'Someone's got it in for me, I'd say.'

'Or me,' Connie breathed, her heart starting to pound. This was clearly the work of whoever it was who'd been trying to scare her with the notes and the graffiti – but this was a whole new level of harassment. Someone could have been seriously hurt; who knew what could have happened when the boat lost power? As it was, she'd lost a day's earnings from the boat tour. That was, in itself, a threat to her livelihood. The notes and graffiti were upsetting, but if she or any of her passengers were actually endangered, it became another thing altogether.

'Oo'd want ter 'urt you, maid?' Uncle Bill blinked owlishly at Connie through his thick spectacles. 'Naw, this'll be about somethin' I did, 'ere or there. Fishermen can be funny buggers. Old grudges, old arguments. Place like this, people 'angs on to an argument. Look at your great-great grandmother Biddy. She 'ad that feud with Rosemary Connor. Connor family still 'ates us, 'cos of it.'

'Do they?' Connie was temporarily distracted. 'Who? I only know Ellen, and she seems very friendly.'

'Ellen? Oh. One of Fred's daughters. Aye well, mebbe she's forgiven us. Fred 'asn't started likin' me, though. 'Ee still ignores me at the pub.'

Connie thought of telling Uncle Bill about her and Ellen laying flowers on Biddy and Rosemary's graves, but thought better of it, if Bill was still entrenched in some kind of feud.

'Now then, let's not jump to conclusions.' The constable got up and adjusted his parka hood in the rain. 'Connie, let's go back to your house and I'll take yer statement.'

'Why, what happened between you and Fred?' Connie felt the rain starting to leak inside the mac. She didn't want to be outside:

she had the feeling of being watched again, even though there was only her, Adrian, Uncle Bill and the coastguard in the harbour now. Her heart beating hard, she scanned the cove, but she couldn't see anyone. However, that didn't mean that no one was there.

'Ah, it was a long time ago. Fell out over a woman.' Uncle Bill allowed himself to be guided off the *Pirate Queen*, with Connie holding his arm as he stepped down gingerly off the ramp. 'History repeats itself, I s'pose, what with Biddy losing her Sam to Rosemary Connor. Still, 'twas the other way around wi' me an' Fred Robb. 'Is mother was a Connor, see. Anyway, Fred was courtin' your auntie Maggie when I met 'er, but we fell in love and she married me. Fred 'ated me ever since.'

'You think Fred Robb took the clamps off the fuel line on the *Pirate Queen*?' Connie asked in disbelief as they walked with Constable Chalmers over the wet sand in the cove, past the Hughes beach house and up towards the steps off the beach.

Bill patted her arm. 'Dunno, maid. But 'oo else would? I cain't imagine anyone 'avin a grudge against a lovely thing like you.'

I can imagine it, though, Connie thought. *I can imagine it all too clearly, though I have no idea why.*

'I don't know,' she replied; it was no more than the truth. She had no idea who would be out to get her, or why – but it seemed that someone in Magpie Cove still hated her.

'In cases like these, where there's ongoin' harassment, best to report every incident. You're doing the right thing, my love,' Constable Chalmers said as they turned onto the end of Connie's mum's cottage.

Uncle Bill sucked on his pipe. 'You'll be 'appy to see my sister, Adrian. Never known you get down to a call so quick as earlier. Anyone'd think you were sweet on 'er.'

'I'm just doin' my job, as it 'appens.' Adrian blushed under his parka. 'I take my police work seriously, I'll 'ave you know, Bill Christie.'

Uncle Bill caught Connie's eye and gave her a grin. She knew that her uncle was trying to take her mind off what had happened, so she smiled back, and followed them into the cottage. Yet, when Adrian had taken hers and Uncle Bill's statements and had left, she went up to her room and stared out of her window onto the street. Who hated her this much, and why?

23

Connie was standing in the lunch queue at Serafina's when Alex tapped her on the arm. She jumped involuntarily; her nerves were on edge.

'Hey. Whoa, steady. You're up and about, then? Feeling okay?' he asked, giving her a cautious smile. He looked good today, although he always did: however, today, unlike his usual casual shirts and jeans, he was wearing a well-cut black suit with a light blue shirt. 'Sorry, I didn't mean to startle you. Just... I was worried about you. You didn't reply to my texts much.'

'Hi. Yeah, sorry about that...' Connie nodded, not knowing what to say. Alex knew what had happened – everyone did, probably, by now. 'Just having some lunch with Mum.'

Connie had reluctantly agreed to meet Esther at Serafina's for some lunch, since her mother had claimed the day before that *I fancy a bit o' quality time with my darlin' girl.* Connie wasn't fooled: she knew it was Esther's way of getting her out of the house. She hadn't left home for the past week, pretending to have a headache, but really, she was shaken up from the boat incident. Until now, the notes had upset her, but someone messing with the boat was much more serious. She was lucky that no one had been hurt. The whole situation had gone from a bit upsetting to deeply worrying and she wasn't sure she was handling it that well.

'You don't need to apologise: I was just worried, that's all.' Alex still looked concerned. 'Is the boat okay?'

'It's fine. Thanks. Someone removed the clamps on the fuel line, so halfway into the trip, I lost power at sea. Coastguard came and towed us in but I had to give refunds to all the customers.'

Her mum and Uncle Bill both seemed convinced that the problem with the *Pirate Queen*'s fuel line was caused by some local with a grudge against Bill, or possibly 'kids', which was their catch-all to explain anything that went wrong.

'Bloody hell. That's awful.' Alex hugged her. 'You don't deserve that. I'm so sorry.' It was comforting being in his arms, but she stepped away, automatically putting distance between them. She didn't quite know why she did it, only that she didn't like the idea of everyone in Magpie Cove knowing her business. One hug from Alex and the rumour mill would be in full swing overnight. *Were they courting? Were they engaged?* Connie hated that about Magpie Cove. She missed Plymouth, where nobody had any interest in her personal life. However, she noted the disappointment in his eyes as she stepped away, and she wondered if avoiding gossip was really more important than letting Alex comfort her. She'd pushed him away all week, but she didn't know how to be in a relationship with Alex yet. What was wrong with letting people know they'd started seeing each other? She didn't really have an answer.

'Who do you think it was? Cheeky so-and-sos... if I get hold of them, they'll regret picking on you,' he muttered darkly.

'I don't know. But look, can we talk about this later?' Connie reached the counter and gave her order to Lila behind the till.

'Okay. Well, I won't get in your way, just came in for a coffee. I'm glad I saw you though...' he looked slightly awkward, 'I was wondering... if you'd like to go out again? There's a new restaurant in St Ives I've heard good things about. Plus, I heard the chef might be leaving so I was going to check out her food, and then maybe see if she was interested in working for me. Only if you're feeling up to it, of course.'

Connie felt a stab of anxiety in her stomach.

'Oh, I don't know... maybe. Let me think about it?' she hedged. She knew she should say yes, but she still felt fragile and paranoid. Was someone watching her now, in the café? There was no way of knowing. Rationally, she knew that an evening in St Ives with Alex was unlikely to cause any problems, but her instinct was to run home and lock the door after her.

Connie shot a look at her mum who was watching her and Alex expectantly.

Connie had tried, again, to talk to her mum about feeling she was being stalked, but Esther had stroked her daughter's hair affectionately and told her not to worry. Connie didn't know if she was deliberately playing everything down for Connie's sake, perhaps in an attempt not to worry her, but Connie wished that Esther would take it all a bit more seriously.

As if I was a child, Connie thought, angrily. She loved Esther, but all of this was just like being a teenager and being hustled into Esther's matchmaking schemes – she wasn't listened to then, and she wasn't listened to now.

'Mum thinks it's all a run of bad luck or something. However...' she broke off and looked over at Esther, who was frantically beckoning and making complicated movements with her hands that Connie interpreted as *bring Alex over here so I can assess him as your future husband*. 'I think I'm supposed to take you over there. If I don't, my life won't be worth living.'

'Okay, but I do have to head off.' Alex waved at Esther and took the takeaway coffee Lila handed him. He took her hand and squeezed it. 'Come on. Come out with me. You could do with a night out. And I'd like to pick up where we left off...' he leaned in towards her and kissed her, sudden and out of the blue. 'I missed you,' he muttered.

'Okay.' Connie had that same feeling as before, as if they were the only people in the world. Alex was the only person she'd ever kissed that made her feel that way. 'I'll come. Thank you.'

'No need to thank me. I've been dying to see you. Much more fun than this meeting I'm off to, also,' he sighed. 'I've got an appointment with the council about the cliff edge. I spoke to a different surveyor, and you're right. It is a problem.'

'Oh. Sorry.'

'Nothing to feel sorry for. You were there, the other night. It's dangerous. Did you know, by the way, that we also had two cars that same night with their windscreens smashed in? Something in the air that night, I guess.'

'Oh, goodness. No, I didn't know.' Connie had got a taxi home after helping Alex sort everything out, as Ellen had given her a lift up to the pub but had then disappeared. 'That's terrible.'

'Yeah. It was a strange old night. I was surprised to see you out with Ellen Robb, by the way. I forgot to say this at the time.' Alex broke into a smile for Esther as they approached the table. 'You know she's a bit... odd, like?'

Connie frowned at him, but he was greeting Esther and there wasn't an opportunity to ask what he meant by Ellen being odd – she assumed it was just the fact that Ellen could be a bit socially awkward, but she felt like she'd got beyond that a little, particularly after their recent trip to the churchyard.

'Connie! I never knew you and Alex were such good friends.' Esther clucked affectionately. 'Oooh, you're well over six feet tall, aren't you, Alex? That was a lovely party, up at the pub. I do 'ope you've got plans to take my Connie out on a proper date. Lovely girl, she is. Clever, too. Not just a pretty face.'

Connie wondered if there was any way she could escape the conversation, if not by the somewhat cliched disappearing into a hole in the floor, then perhaps just running out of the café, but Esther grabbed her arm and made her sit down.

'I know how smart your daughter is, Esther. And how beautiful.' Alex smiled gently at Connie. 'And I just asked her out again, so you don't have to worry.'

'Oooh, again? I didn't know you'd already been on a date! She never tells me anythin', Alex. Mind you, she's a good girl, not like some I could mention. First some kid goes an' knackers poor Bill's boat, just for a laugh, and then I 'eard Fred Robb's daughter's gone up and left the village. Overnight! Just like that.' She snapped her fingers. 'Can you imagine?' Esther sat back in her seat with a satisfied look on her face. 'Always a bit funny, though, that family.'

'What do you mean, left her flat? Left Magpie Cove altogether?' Connie frowned. Ellen hadn't said anything about moving. They'd just seen each other a week ago.

'It's Nathan what owns that flat they live in, you know, Serafina's son. What owns this place now.' Esther waved her hand at the café. 'Never a borrower nor a lender be, that's my advice. Nor a landlord.' She sniffed, disapprovingly.

'It's not 'ow it used to be,' Esther insisted. 'Our 'ouse been ours since we moved from the big 'ouse, oooh, that was generations back. Time was the young 'uns take over the 'ouse when the old 'uns die. We looked after our own, we did: never asked for 'elp. Nowadays, though, it's all different. No fishin'. Everyone 'as to move away for work. Which is why I'm so 'appy Connie came back, and now she's met a lovely local boy.' Esther clapped her hands. 'That's made my year, that 'as.'

'Well, let's not count our chickens before they're hatched, Mum.' Connie blushed again. 'Anyway, I think Alex has to go now.'

'Oh, no.' Esther looked disappointed. ''Ee's got time to sit down for a bit, I'm sure.'

Alex looked at his watch, then sat down next to Esther. 'I'm sure I can spare five minutes.'

'Connie! Pull up a chair and sit. You're making me feel like I'm on trial,' Esther tutted, before turning back to Alex. 'So, my love. Pub goin' well, is it?'

'It's going very well, thanks, Mrs Christie. Just some land issues to sort out, but we're getting lots of bookings for parties, weddings, that kind of thing. Very romantic, up there on the cliffs.' He shot a half-amused glance at Connie, who frowned at him in reply. At this rate, Esther would have them married off by the end of lunch.

'Oooh, I can imagine!' Esther cooed. 'Perfect for your weddin'. I can see it now: a rose arch, flower girls in pink dresses, dancin' in the garden. I'll start lookin' for a hat.'

'Mum!' Connie exclaimed, blushing bright red.

Alex laughed. 'Well, it's early days, Mrs Christie,' he said, his cheeks colouring pink. Yet, unlike Connie, he didn't seem uncomfortable at the thought at all.

'Look, I'm sorry to rain on everyone's parade, but we have only been on one date so far, so can we just rein it in a bit, please?' Connie exclaimed.

Esther tutted. 'Oh, she can be a right wet blanket sometimes, Alex.'

'Please don't talk about me like I'm not here, Mum.'

'Can we just go back to Ellen for a minute?' Alex drummed his fingers on the table. 'I was just thinking... you don't think it's her that's been doing all those things? Not Hazel?'

'Funny maid, that Ellen.' Esther looked disapproving. 'Who d'you mean, Hazel? Hazel Goody, what went to school with you?'

'Mum, I know you don't want to think about it, but ever since I've been back, you know someone's been harassing me. Following me, sending me weird notes. Then there was the message on the museum door, and now the boat.' Connie frowned. 'I thought it might be Hazel. I sent her a message asking her if it was, and I was going to ask her in person but she's disappeared as well. But it can't be Ellen. We've made friends. She's actually nice.'

'What if it was Ellen? Surely making friends with you would all be part of the plan, wouldn't it? Sort of lull you into a false sense of security. Keep your friends close and your enemies closer, that kind of thing.'

Connie thought about it, but it didn't feel quite right, even though everything Alex was saying made a sort of backwards sense. Ellen had seemed to lock onto her and be super keen to be friends, despite the fact that Connie didn't remember her at all from school, or even be that friendly towards her.

'Ellen Robb?' Esther tutted. 'She's always been a bit funny, like. But I'm not sure she'd do any of them things, darlin'. Never struck me as a maid what'd know their way around a boat engine, neither. Not enough to know about the clamps on the fuel line. Mind you, I could say the same for Hazel. Not one to get 'er 'ands dirty. An' she's got them fake nails anyway. They'd be murder on a boat engine.'

'Ellen was at the pub when the car windscreens got smashed.' Alex exchanged glances with Connie. 'You've got to have a bit of a temper to do that. Same as being vengeful enough to scratch nasty messages on people's doors.'

'Most of the village was there that night. Doesn't prove anything,' Connie interjected.

'Connie, my love, I've told you. You're just bein' paranoid, just like when you was a teenager. There's no one out ter get yer. It's just bad luck,' Esther repeated.

'Doesn't it seem like a bit of a coincidence to you that Ellen's disappeared suddenly from the village just after someone scuppered the *Pirate Queen*?' Connie asked her mother.

'It's just a coincidence, maid. Now, just leave it alone. I wish I'd never mentioned it.'

Alex ran a hand through his black hair. 'I guess she could have done the windscreens, but why would she?'

'I don't know. She was a bit funny when she found out we'd been on a date. I think she has a bit of a crush on you.' Connie was thinking back to her conversations with Ellen. 'Maybe she was more upset about it than she let on. I really don't know her that well.'

'Not a lot to know.' Esther swatted her hand, as if there was an invisible fly nearby. 'She lives with 'er sister, whatsername. Junie. That one's trouble, I can tell you. Bill 'ad to ban 'er from the museum a year ago. Tried to steal a model ship. No idea what for, mind. She probably didn't know either.'

'Ellen told me she made greetings cards for a living. I remember, because it seemed so unlikely anyone could live on that,' Connie said.

'First I've 'eard of it,' Esther scoffed. 'Mind you, maybe she did. Both 'er and 'er sister never 'eld jobs down long, though. I know because Fred's always moanin' in the pub about payin' for everythin'. Don't seem ter stop 'im drinkin' the 'ousekeepin' money away every Friday, mind. Ellen's better than Junie, but she still always seemed troubled to me.'

'Is this what you meant earlier, when you said you didn't know why we were hanging out together?' Connie asked Alex, who shrugged. 'Because Ellen was "troubled"?' She made quote marks in the air, mimicking her mother's phrase.

'Kinda. I mean, it's up to you who your friends are. But I did wonder. Ellen and Junie are a bit strange, I always thought.' He looked concerned. 'Look, if you want to talk about this later, give me a call. Okay?'

'Okay.' Connie didn't know what to think. She really didn't want to believe that Ellen, who had become her friend, would do this to her. But she had to consider the possibility that Alex was right.

He got up and buttoned his suit jacket. 'Anyway, it's been lovely chatting, Mrs Christie, but I'd better head off.'

'Oh, call me Esther, please. Or Mum!' Esther twinkled, standing up and beckoning Alex down to her five-foot-one level and planting a kiss on his cheek.

'Esther's fine for now.' Alex tried to catch Connie's eye. 'Connie, I'll pick you up tomorrow night at seven, then?'

'Sure,' Connie replied.

'Connie! Say goodbye properly!' Esther scolded, slapping her daughter's hand. 'Poor Alex won't want to take you out if you're going to act like a sulky teenager.'

'Mum, will you just leave it!' Connie shouted, and stalked out of the café, past a bewildered Alex and into the street. Almost instantly, she felt stupid for losing her temper, but her mother really wound her up sometimes, and she'd been worried about the boat all week. It was like Esther cared much more about what other people thought of Connie than about her own daughter's feelings.

She looked back at the café and saw Alex walking towards the door. Not knowing what to say, she walked stiffly down the street and ducked into one of the narrow alleys to avoid him. Somehow, a casual lunch with her mother had turned into a drama. She was embarrassed at her outburst; it made her look childish, and Alex was probably rethinking asking her out on another date already. Who would want to spend time with a woman that had blazing rows with her mother in public?

As Connie stood in the alley, another thought occurred to her. If Ellen had been behind all of the things that had happened to her since she'd come back to Magpie Cove, she must also have been the one that had harassed her as a teenager. Had Ellen Robb really hated her for all this time? She'd been kind of prepared to believe it was Hazel, but Ellen? It seemed worse, somehow, to think that there was someone who hated her so passionately and she'd never even been aware of their existence.

Connie felt tears spring to her eyes, and wiped them away furiously.

Maybe coming back to Magpie Cove had been a mistake.

She looked back at her phone, and at the message from Georgia at the theatre. She'd been holding off making a decision about the job because she'd promised her mum she'd make a go of the museum and the boat tours, and – if she was honest – she'd started to feel excited about seeing Alex too.

Watching Alex walk away up the street, Connie's heart broke a little. She didn't want him to go, but what could she say to erase what a fool she'd just been? *Come on,* she pep-talked herself. *Of all the men in all the world, you've got stuck on precisely the type of guy you always said you hated. Would it really be that hard to leave someone you've only gone out on one proper date with?*

If she left, what would happen to the museum? Uncle Bill definitely wasn't up to running it anymore, or taking tourists out on the boat. If Connie didn't look after the museum and the *Pirate Queen*, who would?

And, yes, living with her mother at her age was really, really irritating. Esther was strong as a horse, but Bill was getting on, and Connie could see that it wouldn't be long until he needed more care. Bill was still stubbornly refusing to move out of his house on the cove, but he already found the stairs pretty difficult. If Connie moved away now, she knew she'd worry about both of them.

She looked at the message one more time and put the phone back in her pocket. She'd make a decision tomorrow.

24

'So, I'm hoping that the cliff side around the pub can get added to Coastal Cornwall's preservation scheme. Otherwise, it looks like I'm going to have to close *The Lookout* altogether. That's what my surveyor recommended. I've got to do an application. Bloody pages long. Not my strong suit,' he grumbled, then caught Connie's eye. 'Sorry. Listen to me. It's not very sexy, is it? Talking about coastal erosion on a date.'

'I think I mentioned it on our first date.'

Alex raised an eyebrow. 'Touche.'

It had been a lovely dinner, and Connie gazed happily at the fairy lights strung over the fronts of the restaurants as they walked along the beachfront in St Ives. There were even lights along the masts of the sailing ships in the harbour, which shone softly on the water.

'No, it's okay. I don't mind. This is important stuff, anyway.' Connie was glad she'd put her anxiety to one side and come out after all, though a few glasses of wine had definitely helped quiet her mind too. 'It's your business on the line.'

'Yeah. Well, anyway, I'll do the form and send it in and then I guess, keep my fingers crossed.' Alex's hand brushed hers as they

walked, and his touch sent little pinpricks of excitement up
Connie's arm. 'Thanks for coming out tonight.'

The moon was waning – it had been a couple of weeks since
their first night under the stars together – and the summer night
was warm, with a clear dusky blue sky still. The nights were slowly
getting darker again, but most nights were still light until nine-
thirty or so.

'Thanks for asking me. Especially after yesterday at the café.
You must have thought I was such a brat.' Connie cringed, thinking
about it. 'It's just that...' she sighed. 'I've just been really stressed.
Since what happened on the boat. And my mother winds me up at
the best of times. I love her, and everything, obviously. But she
never listens to me, and it... after what happened, I just wanted her
to believe me. Ugh, I don't know. All mothers push our buttons
sometimes, right?' She smiled up at Alex, noting that he'd left the
suit from yesterday at home in favour of a more casual outfit, but
he still seemed to be making an effort: he was wearing jeans, but
smart ones, and a nice shirt with a blue pattern that looked like a
designer label.

She'd agonised about what to wear, not being much of a
dressy girl – she'd got used to jeans and T-shirts at uni and then
at work, which could often involve painting sets at the last
minute, moving heavy furniture and all manner of other manual
tasks; the museum and the *Pirate Queen* didn't exactly require
anything fancy in terms of dress, either. In the end, she'd settled
on an old dress of Esther's – not the shocking pink one, but a little
black number with thin shoulder straps and a pencil skirt to the
knee. It was simple, but it fitted well and showed off her petite
figure.

She'd texted him that morning, apologising for walking out of
the café in a huff and saying it was fine if he wanted to cancel their
date. He'd replied:

Don't be daft. Pick you up at 7xx

'Bloody hell. *Yes.* Mine's the same, anyway. Maybe it's a Cornish thing.'

Connie rolled her eyes. 'I think it's just a mother thing.' Alex took her hand casually.

'Don't worry. And of course you're going to be on edge after what happened. She just wants the best for you, though.'

'Oh. And you're the best, are you?' she teased.

'Naturally.' Alex pulled her in close to him and, without any preamble, kissed her.

It was a good, deep kiss that started softly, but both of them felt its urgency grow as the seconds passed. Connie wrapped her arms around Alex's neck, standing on tiptoe to reach his lips; in return, he held her lightly around the waist, almost lifting her up. Despite the fact that she still felt a little anxious, Connie imagined being lifted up and wrapping her legs around his waist, kissing him, and maybe more... and her heart beat faster at the thought. There was a crackling, hot chemistry between them.

Gently, he released her from her arms and Connie's feet made contact with the pavement again, grounding her. Still, she took a few moments to come back to earth.

She cleared her throat. 'Well, then.'

'Hmmm.' Alex grinned at her, and took her hand again. 'D'you want more of a walk, or... We could go back to the pub. I haven't showed you my flat up there yet.'

He was gazing into her eyes, and Connie could feel the pull of attraction towards him like she was a boat caught in a strong tide.

She wanted to go. Everything in her body was yelling *yes, yes, go, be with Alex*, because they both knew what he was suggesting. They'd fooled around, that night on the cliff, and even fallen asleep in each other's arms, but they hadn't slept together then.

She wanted to, and there was no reason why she shouldn't. It felt right. It had felt right since the day she ran into him on the street, if she was honest with herself. Her body wanted Alex Gordon, and she knew he wanted her.

Yet, if she was going back to Plymouth, it didn't make sense to get more involved with him now. It would just make everything messier. She'd been thinking more and more about Georgia's offer, and it seemed like the only sensible solution. Despite the lovely evening in St Ives they were having, this wasn't Magpie Cove. In St Ives, Connie didn't need to be careful, and she could let herself relax a little. In St Ives, she wasn't always looking over her shoulder, waiting for the next attack. And that's how it was now. Since the boat had been tampered with, she just couldn't relax and feel happy in the village anymore.

Could she ever have a happy relationship with anyone in that environment? Could she ever relax and be Alex's girlfriend if she was always stressed? Wouldn't he start to get tired of it, too, after a time?

She didn't want that. As much as she liked Alex, and as much as her body was screaming at her, *just kiss him, go back with him now, you'll regret it if you don't*, she knew it wouldn't be right.

She let go of his hand and took a step away.

'I think maybe I'll just go home, if that's okay with you,' she heard herself saying.

'Go home? I mean... sure, of course. Is anything wrong? I thought...' he trailed off. 'I thought we were having a good time.'

'We were. We are. I just... I just want to go,' she repeated, feeling wretched. 'The thing is... I've accepted a job offer, back in Plymouth. Well, I haven't accepted, but I'm going to. I'm leaving. So... I don't think it's a good idea to get more involved right now.' She felt the words hang between them in the air like some kind of curse.

Bewilderment filled Alex's face.

'A job? What about the museum? You can't just leave.'

'I'll help Mum find someone else. I have to go. I want to go,' she insisted.

'But... I thought we were... this is good, between us. I don't want you to go.'

Connie's heart wrenched: he looked so disappointed.

'We've only been on a couple of dates, Alex. What... did you want to get married, settle down? I'm not going to be your good little wifey, you know, no matter what my mother thinks.'

'I never thought that. I like the fact you're independent. I just want you to be around, so we can get to know each other.' He caught her hand. 'Connie, please.'

She was intentionally being cruel; there was something in her heart that felt as though, if she was awful to him, it would be kinder on him in the long run. More like pulling a bandage off quickly. But she couldn't stand the look on his face.

'Please, Alex. Don't make this more difficult than it is,' she pleaded.

'I'm not making it difficult. You've just brought this up out of nowhere. We were just having a nice evening, and then, bam! *Bye, Alex. Nice knowing you.* I've got feelings, you know.' He turned away, folding his arms over his chest.

'You can come and see me in Plymouth, you know. It's not the other side of the world.' She touched his back, gently.

'Might as well be,' he muttered, sulkily, not turning around. 'You know I work long days at the pub. I hardly get a day off. When am I supposed to get all the way up there?'

'Well, you'd make time if you really wanted to,' she countered, annoyed at his sudden sulkiness. 'And can you look at me when I'm talking to you, please?'

'I can't just pull time out of thin air,' he grumbled, turning back to face her. 'Be reasonable, Connie.'

'You're not listening, Alex,' Connie tried again. What would it take to get him to understand? 'This is hard for me, you know. It's not a decision I'm taking lightly.'

'Feels like it.' He looked away, out over the marina. 'Why take a job when you've already got one here?'

'It's hard to explain,' she said, evasively.

'Is it because of what happened at the museum? The notes and stuff? You shouldn't leave because of that.' Connie knew he didn't mean it to sound like an accusation of weakness on her part, but that was how it felt, and her defences went up.

'Oh, really? Why shouldn't I? If you'd ever been victimised just for being yourself – for existing, as a woman, in a way that some crazy person didn't like – then you'd know it's the perfectly sensible thing to do,' she countered, angrily. 'Don't you dare tell me what I should and shouldn't do. And what happened on the boat wasn't kids' stuff. That was dangerous. What if someone gets hurt next time? Or I get hurt?'

'Connie, that's not what I meant. I meant... don't let them win. That's what they want, presumably. For you to leave. Please.' He took her hand and tried to pull her into an embrace. 'Please don't go. I'll protect you. I'll be with you night and day. They won't dare touch you if I'm around.'

Connie pulled her hand away from his. She knew he meant well, but she was getting desperate: she knew she had to leave, and if she couldn't make Alex understand, then she had to make him let her go another way.

'Alex. Please.' She felt tears welling up in her eyes. Her throat felt tense, almost sore, with the pressure of her emotions. 'You can't protect me forever, and I wouldn't want you to. I don't want to live a life in fear, always having to have you around. What would you do? Give up your job to be my personal bodyguard? It's a crazy idea.'

'We'd make it work. You could work at the pub. Move into my flat. I could keep an eye on you.'

'Alex, I'm not going to do those things. You do know that, right? That's bordering on obsessive. I don't want to work in your pub. And, moving in together? When we've only just started going out? That's mad.' Connie wrapped her arms around herself in an unconscious gesture of self-protection. Alex's solution to her problem was just ownership in another form. If the stalker wanted to control her, somehow – at least, control her movements and make her scared to go out – then Alex's instinct was similar, even though he wanted to protect her. Neither was healthy: neither was what she wanted.

'I just want to be free,' Connie said in a low voice, trying not to let her emotions take over altogether. 'I want to live somewhere I don't feel watched. I want to enjoy my job. I don't want to feel like I need you to protect me. As far as I can see, the only solution is to move away.'

'Well, what do you want me to do? Walk away? Not going to happen.' Alex's eyes flashed. 'This is good, between us. You know that. You must know how rare it is, to find this. Don't give up on us, Connie. Please.'

He wasn't going to give up on her: Connie could see that. Her heart sank. She knew that the only way she could make the break was to make him hate her: to do or say something so hateful that he could never forgive her. She knew what she would say, and gathered the sentence in her mind. Her throat constricted, as if it was trying to stop her.

'Anyway, I'd expect a man who once got a restraining order to make a bit more of an effort. You must be losing it. Or maybe you don't like me as much as you liked your ex.'

As soon as she said it, she knew she'd gone too far, and her heart ached. But it was too late, and she watched the reaction on Alex's face as her words hit him.

'What did you just say?' He took a couple of steps back from her, frowning now. 'I told you. I didn't get a restraining order. She just threatened me with it. I told you that in confidence as something that was really hard for me to talk about. Yes, I've made mistakes in the past, but I've moved on and learned from them. But thanks for throwing that back in my face at the first opportunity.'

'Yeah, well, maybe it's just as well I'm leaving.' Connie turned away so that he couldn't see the tears in her eyes. She thought if she looked at him, she would start sobbing and he'd know she hadn't meant it. That, somehow, in a very misguided way, she'd been trying to be kind. 'I'll get a taxi back, don't worry about having to drop me home.'

'Fine.' He reached into his pocket and pulled out his wallet.

'I don't need you to pay,' Connie's voice squeaked.

Alex stared at her for a moment, then pulled a business card from his wallet and handed it to her.

'I know that. This is a taxi firm I use. If you mention my name, they'll come for you in ten minutes. Heaven forbid I should try to be a gentleman. See you around.' With that, he stalked off.

Connie watched him go, her heart in her mouth. She wanted to run after him. She wanted to apologise for being so cruel, but she couldn't make her feet move. Despite it being awful, she felt like she'd done the right thing. She'd only end up hurting him more if she spent the night with him now, she knew that. But it was hard, watching him walk away.

Connie called the number on the card Alex had given her: sure enough, someone answered immediately, and she only had to wait a few minutes until the taxi arrived.

Once inside, she tried to hide the fact that she was crying, but she obviously didn't do a great job because the taxi driver handed her a tissue box, wordlessly, as he drove along the dark country roads leading back to Magpie Cove.

25

Connie sat on her bed and stared at the empty suitcase next to her.

She'd just got off the phone to Georgia: the job as stage manager on *Uncle Vanya* was hers. She'd have to be back in Plymouth in a week.

She could leave Magpie Cove.

She could leave Esther's meddling behind, and have some space to herself.

She could go back to the job she'd always really loved, and to the theatre community, where no one knew her as one of the Christie family. Where she could just be Connie.

Connie went over to her chest of drawers, which had been repainted a plain white by Esther so many times that the drawers no longer shut properly. She opened the top drawer and started taking her underwear out, tossing it into the suitcase.

It shouldn't be that hard to leave Alex, but somehow, it was. Her heart hurt at the thought of it, like there was some kind of rubber band attaching her to him. She thought of how it felt when he held her in those huge arms: he was like some kind of kindly bear, though the look he sometimes gave her under his eyelashes definitely didn't feel comforting. That was something else entirely.

Then, she thought about the night before again, and her heart broke as she remembered his expression when they'd argued. She'd been so awful to him, and on purpose, too. She'd wanted to make it easier: make it easier for him to let her go. She didn't want to be connected to him, didn't want that tidal pull that made her want to run to him tonight and apologise, to run into his arms and kiss him like they'd kissed in St Ives the night before. It made everything too complicated.

She glanced out of the window: she hadn't closed the curtains yet, since it was still so light outside on these summer evenings. As she moved towards the window to pull them shut, her eye was drawn to something moving on the street opposite the house.

Connie leaned closer to the glass, frowning. It was the shadow of a person – no – not a shadow, a person, dressed in dark clothing. She couldn't see their face.

She drew back from the window a little, watching. Whoever it was had seen her, she could tell: they stood completely still, but their posture showed that they were looking up at her. Connie's heart began to race.

Was it Ellen, out there, watching her? Or Hazel?

Bravely, she pushed up the window and leaned out.

'Hey! I can see you, you know! Leave me alone!'

The figure crossed its arms over its chest, appearing defiant. It didn't move.

'Who's there? Why are you doing this?' Connie yelled, feeling her temper rise. She was still afraid, but she was also angry. 'Hazel, is that you? What have I done to you? What did I do wrong? Ellen? Show me your face!'

The figure shook its head, but said nothing.

'Right.' Connie stepped back from the window. She was going down there, and she was going to confront whoever it was, face to face.

But before Connie could get down the stairs, she heard the front door swing open and her mother's voice shout:

'Hey! You! What you up to? You watchin' my 'ouse? Are yer? Bloody cheek!'

Connie ran down the stairs to find Esther, armed with a broom, running out of the house at full pelt at the figure on the street.

'Mum!' she shouted after Esther, but Esther was not to be distracted. Connie grabbed a set of keys, pulled the front door shut after her and ran after her mother, who was now pursuing the stalker down their road. 'Mum! Leave it!' Connie shouted, aware that she didn't have any shoes on. Esther did, at least, but Connie was afraid her mum would fall over any minute. The fact she was running at all was remarkable, given that she had a pretty stiff hip.

But Esther plunged on, waving her broom, and at the end of the road, ran into a surprised Alex Gordon.

'Come back 'ere , bloody nuisance!' she panted.

'Esther! What on earth...' he caught the wild-eyed Cornish-woman and steadied her. 'Connie! I was just coming to see you. I wanted to talk, about last night...' he trailed off, looking confused. 'Why are you and your mother running around the streets at this time of night?'

Connie had caught up to them both. She pointed at the figure in black who had run towards the cove.

'That's my stalker. Mum saw them outside the house and ran after them. I was running after Mum,' she explained, out of breath.

'That's your stalker? Right. Come on. I've had enough of this.' Alex turned around and broke into a run. 'I'm not letting them get away this time,' he shouted over his shoulder.

Connie handed the house keys to her mother.

'Mum. Go home and call the police. I'm going with Alex. OK?' She looked pleadingly at her mother.

'Right ye are. Go dreckly, or you'll lose 'em.' Esther used the old Cornish word for *quickly*. She took the keys and shooed her daughter away. 'I'll call 999.'

Connie nodded and sprinted after Alex, hoping she could still follow. As she chased through an alley and onto the sea front, she saw him on the beach, running past the Hughes house and onto the rocks. Her heart tugged in her chest. She wanted to shout *be careful, please be careful, Alex*, but she knew he wouldn't hear her.

She raced down the old stone steps onto the beach, her heart in her mouth. She didn't want Alex to fall on the rocks, but it was more than that. If they caught the stalker, she could end all this. She could live a normal life again. The thought sustained her as she ran, feeling the tiredness in her legs and the burn in her lungs.

Connie *did* really want to stay in Magpie Cove, and catching Hazel – or whoever it was that had escalated things from a few worrying notes to events that could have really hurt Connie, and other people – seemed like something she had to do to make life good here. She'd forgotten, recently, what it could feel like, stepping outside of her door in the morning and not thinking about anything but the day ahead and the sunlight on the calm blue sea Hope filled her heart, chasing out the fear. She could do this.

26

Out of breath, her legs feeling like they were on fire, Connie caught up to Alex. He was standing on top of a pile of slick granite slabs, close to where the cove started to reach into the sea on the left-hand side.

It had been hard to climb up to where he was and not slip, especially in just her socks, but he'd climbed down and helped her up the last part of the way.

She wanted to ask him if he was all right – he'd come looking for her, and he'd said he wanted to talk about the night before. Yet now wasn't exactly the right time to get into a deep conversation about their feelings. Connie put that conversation to the back of her mind and made herself focus in the waning light.

'What's that?' she panted, looking down at the cliff side. Now that they were standing where they were, she could see that there was a dry little alcove below, with a hole in the side of the cliff.

'I dunno, but whoever it was we're chasing, they went in there and they haven't come out.' Alex grimaced. 'I think it might be the entrance to an old tunnel.'

'What, a *smuggling* tunnel?' Connie tried to get her breath. She gave Alex a quizzical look. 'You can't be serious.'

'I am serious. That's not a random hole. Look at it.' He held out his hand for hers, and guided her down the slippery rocks to the sandy ground. 'Look. That's old brick around the edge. You can still see some of it.' He shone the torch on his phone at the cliffside. Sure enough, Connie could see the bricks around the top of the tunnel entrance.

'No way. I thought all these were lost or bricked up.' Her eyes widened in disbelief. 'Uncle Bill never told me about this. Or Dad.'

'They might not have known, I suppose. Or, if they did, maybe they didn't tell you on purpose. They probably knew any kid that knew there was an old open smuggling tunnel around here would go looking for it. Not exactly safe.'

'Did you know about it?' Connie stepped forward gingerly and looked inside. 'Bloody hell. It is. Someone's in there, then. What should we do? Go in?'

'Call the police and tell them where we are. I'm going in.' Alex handed her his phone. 'I'm going to catch this joker. I'm not having any more of this,' he muttered, grimly.

'Alex! You can't go in there!' Connie cried. 'It's not safe. The ceiling could cave in at any minute. Plus, you're massive. You'll never fit. It makes more sense for me to go in.' Connie handed his phone back to him.

'No way. You are not going in there.' Alex pressed 999 on his phone and then the call button. 'Stay there.' He started speaking to the call handler, explaining where they were and that they were pursuing someone they believed had been stalking Connie.

Connie peered inside the tunnel entrance. Probably, the stalker hadn't got far and was hiding in there, listening to everything they said and waiting for them to leave so they could escape. Well, sod that. She didn't appreciate being told what she could and couldn't do by him; she was going in and Alex couldn't stop her.

Before he'd finished the call, Connie bent her head and shuffled into the tunnel.

She heard Alex swear, but ignored him and walked further in.

Inside, the bottom of the tunnel was wet, which was a worry. That meant that if the tide came back in, she'd be trapped in there and drown. Connie wondered if that was normal for a smuggler's tunnel: could they only ever be used at low tide? Perhaps that was part of their secrecy. She supposed that, at some stage in the past, the smugglers would also have had to disguise the entrance – perhaps with piles of rocks, or even a door.

Connie listened for any noises that would give away the location of the stalker, but it was eerily quiet in the cave, and completely dark. Connie wished she'd had the foresight to snatch her phone on the way out of the house earlier, but at least she'd thought of keys and Esther was, presumably, home by now.

The ceiling of the tunnel was low – made for smaller people, Connie thought. The Cornish were typically small anyway, particularly in the past. Alex was some kind of Viking-esque aberration, though he had the black hair and easily tanned brown skin of a Cornishman.

She felt a hand on her arm and screamed involuntarily.

'Shhh! It's me,' Alex hissed. 'I can't believe you ignored me. It's not safe in here. We need to get out before the whole thing caves in, or the tide comes in and drowns us.'

'Bloody hell, Alex. You scared me to death,' she scolded him. 'The tide won't come back in for another hour. Turn on the light on your phone.' Her voice sounded steadier than she felt.

The white light lit up the tunnel. Connie squinted ahead. Surprisingly, the tunnel stretched quite far – she'd almost expected the stalker to be crouching ahead of her, unable to get past a cave-in.

'Connie. We are not chasing this person any further. Okay?'

'No, Alex. It's not okay.' With difficulty, Connie turned around in the tunnel to face him. It was much easier for her to manoeuvre in the small space than it was for him: she saw he was almost bent double.

'Look. You don't know what it's like, what this person – Hazel, whoever – has made life like recently. Every day I wake up and think, is today going to be the day they scare me again?' She wiped her forehead with one dirty hand, leaving a streak of mud on her skin.

'I don't know what they're going to do next. Are they going to turn up at the museum again? Do you know how horrible it is, knowing that it must be someone in the village, but not knowing who? That it might be someone I see every day? Someone I actually like, even? I am not letting them get away this time, Alex. Because if I don't get to the bottom of this – if I can't stop them, then something really serious might happen. Next time, maybe they mess with the boat and I can't three families back to safety. Okay? I can't deal with that kind of uncertainty anymore.'

Connie's voice broke; the words came tumbling out, but she fought the tears of frustration behind them. She didn't want to cry. She wanted to catch her stalker.

'Okay, okay. Hey. I'm sorry,' Alex apologised. 'I get it. Look, the police are on their way. Let's go a bit further, but we're not likely to catch them now if the tunnel is still open all the way. If the tide comes in in an hour, then we've got about twenty minutes to go into the tunnel and get out again safely before it does. And that's assuming you're right about the tide times,' he added.

'Okay,' Connie agreed, heading further into the tunnel. She had to admit that it was good to have Alex with her, and to be able to see with the light. She didn't think she would have argued so passionately to chase this person in an old tunnel without one.

They plodded on carefully. The tunnel seemed to be leading upwards, which made sense if it led to somewhere in the village. Connie noticed that the ground underfoot was dry now. So, they were out of the way of the tide – but if they wanted to get out, then they still had to get past the lower part of the tunnel which would be flooded when the tide did come in.

'Did you ever go into the tunnel? The one connected to your house, I mean?' Connie spoke up as they fumbled along by the light of the torch. Every now and again she thought she heard a footfall ahead or the sound of someone breathing, but it could just as easily have been her own steps, her own breath.

'No. Tim did, like I said. I was too afraid of what Mum would do if she found out. Plus, it's really spooky in there.' He shivered. 'You know the story about the knockers, right? Mum said there was knockers in there.'

'I assume you mean the Cornish elves that lived in the tin mines,' she replied. The air was thin in the tunnel and she was starting to feel lightheaded.

'Yeah. Being down here, you can sort of understand why the miners used to believe in them.' Alex coughed. 'You feel like the earth could fall in on you at any minute, and you do hear funny noises. Speaking of that, I know it's not the time, but I've looked at that form about the erosion. To Coastal Cornwall? It's like reading ancient Greek. They're going to close me down for sure.'

'Oh, right. You should have asked me to look it over,' Connie chided him.

'Well, I would have, but you were too busy breaking up with me,' Alex said, sounding irritated.

'Well, I can. There's no reason to be petty.'

'Fine.'

'Fine.'

They trudged along a little further.

'There. What was that?' Alex stood still, and Connie instinctively did the same. There *was* a scrabbling noise coming from somewhere.

'It could be anything. A rat. Something like that,' Alex started to say, but Connie shushed him.

They stood at an intersection. The tunnel they had come up reached behind them and divided into two directions ahead.

'We should follow the way that has the freshest air,' Connie started to say, thinking about the most sensible option.

'Connie. It's been twenty minutes,' Alex replied. 'Look...' He held up his phone and showed Connie the time. 'We should really go.'

'Hey!' Connie grabbed the phone and shone the light into one of the tunnels. She'd seen something move; she was sure of it. 'There's someone there!'

There was the sudden sound of feet pounding the earth, and someone ran at Connie and pushed her into Alex.

It went dark; Connie heard Alex swear and grip her arm tightly. Connie realised that Alex must have either dropped his phone or it had run out of charge.

Whoever it was that they'd been following up the tunnel was now running back down it in the dark, and they were left in blackness.

27

Connie dropped to her hands and knees and felt around carefully in the dirt floor of the tunnel for Alex's phone, banging her head on his in the process.

'Ow. Stand up, I can find it easier on my own,' Alex grumbled.

'No. It must be here somewhere...' Connie patted the ground, trying to keep her nerve and not freak out in the dark. It was a wonder that she hadn't had a panic attack already, in fact, but maybe because everything had happened so quickly, she hadn't had time to even think about it. 'Here. I've got it.'

She found his outstretched hands in the dark and placed the phone into them. Weak light filled up the tunnel as he turned the home screen back on.

'Huh. The torch doesn't seem to be working. Dropping it must have damaged it or something. These things are supposed to withstand more than being dropped in a puddle,' he muttered.

'Come on. We need to get out as fast as possible. See if we can catch her outside.' Connie started off back down the tunnel. 'Hopefully the police are there by now and can pick her up.'

'Hope so. Or we've just chased someone up and down a tunnel for no reason,' Alex groaned. 'I'm following you. Don't go too fast. Remember I'm doubled over here.'

The light was much weaker than before as they made their way back down the tunnel, and kept going off intermittently; Alex had to keep pressing the home screen to give them any light at all.

Connie realised how tired she was. Goodness only knew how long they'd been chasing this person for – it felt like hours. She asked Alex what the time was, and he told her it was past eleven. She shivered. It would have been scary being in this old tunnel on a sunny lunchtime, but somehow, it being close to midnight made it even worse. Not that she could tell the difference in here.

She jogged as fast as she could back down the tunnel, but there was no sign of whoever it was they were chasing: Connie hadn't had time to register much about the person as they pushed past her: only that they were dressed in dark clothes and had a hood up as before. She felt reasonably sure that the person was more her size than Alex's. She thought back to seeing them outside her house, earlier. Yes. They weren't as tall as he was. It could definitely be Ellen or Hazel.

The earth underfoot had turned wet again and Connie could hear a rushing noise ahead of her.

'Quickly!' she urged Alex on. A few steps after, she realised she was wading through sea water.

'Connie, the tide...' Alex warned her, but she had no choice but to press on.

The water was quickly up to their ankles and then, as the tunnel dropped again, almost up to Connie's knees. She shivered; it was freezing.

Connie felt a wave of panic start in her abdomen and take over her body. She stopped and put her hand on the tunnel wall.

'I can't...' she breathed, feeling her chest seize up. Her heart was hammering like it had before when this happened, and she felt that familiar feeling of dread overtake her. She would die in this tunnel: she felt sure of it.

'Connie?' Alex's hand found the small of her back. 'Connie. It's okay. Breathe in, breathe out. Remember, in-two-three-four-five-six, out-two-three-four-five-six. Slower. Come on, you can do this.' His voice was deep and calming; she tried to slow her breathing, but she couldn't. It was pitch dark now and the water was reaching her knees. She bent over, instinct taking over. She wanted to crouch, to make herself small.

'Connie. Come on,' Alex repeated. 'We can't stay here. You know we can't.'

'I'm sorry,' she panted, another wave of hot dread passing through her. 'Just go. Leave me here.'

'No way.'

In the darkness, Connie felt Alex lift her into his arms.

'What are you doing?' she cried.

'Just hold on,' he replied, grimly, as he waded out of the tunnel and up the rocks outside, carrying her.

The beach outside was lit up in a cold, fluorescent blue by the flashing light of a police car.

28

There was quite a crowd on the beach, including a hollow-eyed Esther, who ran at Connie as soon as Alex carefully placed her down on the sand.

'Connie! I thought you was a goner! The police told me you were both in there. Oh, thank God you're all right!' Her mother enveloped her in a huge hug that left Connie even more breathless than before.

'Mum, I think I need to sit down,' Connie murmured, feeling faint. There was a part of her that hated acting like some kind of Victorian lady, fainting at dramatic moments. Yet as Esther helped her to a seat on the rocks, away from the incoming tide, Connie reasoned with herself that chasing a stalker through town, onto the beach and into an abandoned smuggling tunnel had been a pretty traumatic experience.

'All right now, my angel? 'Ere, I brought you down a thermos of tea an' an iced bun. After you went harin' off after Alex, I went back 'ome, but I couldn't settle. So I says to Bill, call the police an' tell 'em our Connie's gone racin' off with Alex Gordon after some nutter watchin' our 'ouse. I mean, I know you told 'em already, but just in case. An' when Bill phoned through, they told us you'd gone in the tunnel. What were you thinkin', maid?' Her mother shook

her head in exasperation. 'Your brothers were meant to be the mad
ones, not you. Anyway, so I made some tea and came down to find
yer. 'Opin' you weren't drowned, like.'

'Thanks, Mum.' Connie took the bun that Esther handed her
and the flask lid filled with hot tea. 'I didn't drown, as you can see.'

'You missed all the drama while you was in there, mind!'
Esther tutted, pointing over to the police car that was responsible
for the flashing lights, parked on the small dead-end road at the
edge of the beach. Cat's ice cream truck stood closed to one side.
'Before you came out with Alex, she came tearin' out, and Adrian
and Rob caught 'er. Look. Little so-an'-so. I gave 'er a piece of my
mind, an' all. Watchin our 'ouse, scarin' you to death!' Esther
looked furious.

'Who? Hazel? Ellen?' Connie gulped half the tea in the flask
lid while Esther draped a blanket around her shoulders.

'No, silly! 'Twas Ellen's sister, Junie Robb. Turns out she's
been quite the busy bee tonight. Vandalised poor Alex's pub too
before she came down 'ere and decided to frighten the lights out o'
you.'

'Junie Robb?' Connie was confused. 'I've never even met her
before.'

'Oh, well, seems she knows you.' Esther put her arm around
Connie's shoulders and gave her a squeeze. 'Confessed to messin'
with the *Pirate Queen* not so long ago, when you broke down,
remember? An' doin' the graffiti at the museum.'

'But... why would she do all of that?' Connie stared up the
beach at the police car. She could see a huddled outline of
someone sitting inside the back of the car. *Junie Robb*. Ellen had
mentioned she had a sister, here and there, but she'd always been
evasive with the details. A sister that sometimes needed help.
Junie.

'Jealous of you, I'll wager. In love with you, maybe, in a funny
sort of way.' Esther sighed. Connie frowned. 'What? Stranger
things 'ave 'appened. Love turns people foolish. Your Uncle Bill
stole Auntie Maggie from Junie's dad, so the story goes anyway.

Truth was, Maggie 'ad a lucky escape from Fred Robb. Before 'is wife left 'im – that's Ellen and Junie's mother, you don't remember 'er – I saw 'er covered in bruises more than once. Nasty piece of work, 'ee is.' Esther looked dark.

'Truth be told, men like Fred Robb's the reason why I always wanted ter marry ye off early, maid. Find a nice fella and then never 'ave to worry about all that.'

''Course, you resisted me. Even though I vetted all the local boys. I made friends with all the mothers, asked lots of questions, I vetted those boys. Very thorough, I was.' She watched Alex as he walked across the beach towards them. 'Still, at least you found a good one, at last. An'... I'm sorry, darlin'. You told me so many times you were scared, an' I didn't want ter hear it. I didn't want ter believe anyone would mean those things, I thought it was just spite. I'm sorry for not listenin' to you, Connie.'

'Oh, Mum.' Connie felt tears well up in her eyes and wiped them away with the edge of the blanket. She didn't know what to say.

Alex sat down next to Connie. 'All right?' He tapped her awkwardly on the knee.

'She's coming back to normal, my love.' Esther smiled reassuringly at him. 'I 'ave you to thank for gettin' my darlin' girl out alive, Alex. 'Ere, 'ave a bun. Best I can do right now. An' I need to get this one 'ome to warm up in a minute, when she's got a bit o' energy in 'er,' she added.

'We saved each other.' Alex accepted the cake and ate it in two large bites. 'You know who it was, then? You all right, Connie?' he asked, softly.

'I think I'm okay.' Connie frowned. 'I just don't understand. I've never even met Junie Robb,' she repeated. She just couldn't get it through her head that anyone could hate her as much as Junie apparently did without ever even speaking a word to her. She wasn't convinced by her mother's explanation, either: she very much doubted that whatever Junie felt towards her was love. She must have been the one that left her the notes too, that summer before she left Magpie Cove. Maybe it was some kind of obsession. She'd heard about that kind of thing, but she couldn't imagine why anyone would be obsessed with her.

Adrian, the constable who had taken her statement a few weeks ago, made his way down the beach and joined their huddle on the rocks.

'Now, then. We're going to take Junie into custody now, and I suggest you both get a hot bath and a bed, and then come down to the station in the morning,' he said, gently. 'Been quite a night. I can only assume Mara and Brian must be out, otherwise they'd have our guts for garters for making such a disturbance on the beach tonight,' he added, nodding at the beach house to the edge of the cove.

'What's going to happen to her?' Connie looked back at the police car.

'Depends if you want ter press charges. As it is, she confessed to the criminal damage, so that's likely a suspended sentence an' a fine.'

'Can I see her?' Connie asked.

'Depends.' He shrugged. 'Technically, no, you can't see her. But I can't 'elp it if I didn't manage to stop you runnin' up there.'

If it had been Junie Robb stalking her all those years ago too, there was even more of a need to put an end to all of this once and for all. She stood up.

'I've got to see her.' She knew she'd regret it if she didn't.

'Connie, I'm not sure if that's such a good idea...' Alex put his hand on her arm, but she shook it off.

Her heart beating hard, Connie walk-ran up the beach to where the police car sat on the tiny, dead-end road above.

She walked up to the police car, her heart in her mouth. She leaned into the back seat, and met Junie Robb's ferocious stare.

'Why me?' she asked, searching Junie's face, trying to remember her at all, but Junie could have been a stranger. 'I don't even know you. What did I ever do to you?'

Junie regarded her dispassionately.

'Christies is evil. Dad told me. Everyone knows it. Needs takin' down a peg or two.' She shrugged, as if she was just stating a fact.

'But... you can't possibly believe that's true,' Connie spluttered. 'I'm just a normal person. Evil? In what way am I...' But before she could say any more, Liza, Magpie Cove's policewoman, got out of the front of the police car, took Connie firmly by the shoulders and steered her towards Alex, who had run up the beach after her.

'No, thank you, Miss Christie. We got to observe the law, an' Miss Robb's in custody now,' she said, firmly. 'We'll see you at the station tomorrow.'

'Fine. Okay, okay.' Connie held her hands up in surrender. Someone cleared their throat behind her and she looked around, expecting to see Alex and her mother, but Ellen Robb stood on the road, her cheek sporting a darkening bruise.

29

'I don't want to talk to you.' Connie pushed past her, heading home. She was exhausted, and she wasn't particularly interested in another member of the Robb family telling her she was evil and had it coming.

'Connie. Are you okay? Oh my goodness, I'm so, so sorry.' Ellen looked utterly distraught. 'Are you hurt? Let me explain... please.'

Connie kept walking. 'I'm fine, and you've got nothing to explain.'

'Please, Connie. I didn't do any of this. I didn't know what she was doing, and when I did, I tried to stop her. Please, Connie. Just five minutes.' Ellen ran after her. Connie eyed the bruise on her cheek.

'She did that to you?'

Ellen's hand went to her face in a protective gesture.

'Yes. We had a fight, earlier. She told me she'd vandalised Alex's pub and I told her she shouldn't have done it. She said she did it for me.' Ellen started to cry. 'But... Alex... you have to know, I would never have asked her to do anything like that. Please believe me.'

Alex took Connie's hand, protectively.

'I don't know what to believe, Ellen. I don't think either of us do,' he replied, seriously. 'I'm not going to stand here and pretend I'm not devastated about the fact that your mad sister's destroyed my pub. D'you know how hard I worked on renovating that place? That's my family's money in that building. I don't even want to go up there and see it. I can't bring myself to go, but I have to.' He ran his hand through his black hair. 'When was this, anyway? It must have been before she showed up outside Connie's house earlier. The pub's been closed all day, and I spent the day at my mum and dad's. I haven't even been up there.'

'Oh, I'm so sorry, Alex,' Ellen repeated, wringing her hands. 'I don't know exactly what she did. I told her not to go up there, and we had this fight... she hit me and stormed off and I couldn't stop her. She took Dad's car. I did call the police, but I guess they didn't get there in time.'

'Well, you could have told me – you could have told anyone! – that Junie was violent, before now. When did you find out she'd been stalking Connie?' Alex towered over Ellen, still holding Connie's hand firmly.

'I didn't know. She's always... she disappears, then she comes back and she don't tell you where she's been. The night we went for a drink up at the pub, she was up there then. That was why I went off, Connie, when I was supposed to take you home. She'd put in the windscreens of some of the cars.' Ellen took in a deep breath. 'Thing is, Alex, she knew I had a little crush on you. Like a lot of girls around here. In her way, she was doing it for me. She followed me up there that night; I saw her hanging around. I told her you and Connie were seeing each other and she just blew her top.'

Ellen looked utterly mortified at having to admit it in front of Alex, and Connie found herself feeling sorry for the girl. She looked absolutely exhausted, and it was clear that it hurt her to talk because she grimaced every now and again. Connie wondered if Junie had broken Ellen's cheekbone.

'Bloody hell. That cost me a lot of money, you know. I paid to have those windscreens replaced, to save bad publicity,' Alex fumed. 'Why didn't you tell me then?'

'I should have, but I was mortified that I'd let it happen – and, honestly, I felt terrible that you and Connie'd find out and think worse of me. I left the village. I couldn't cope with Junie no more on my own. I told Dad she was getting worse, but he's always refused any help for her. Thing is, since Mum left, he's been on the drink and he just expects me to look after her, like an unpaid carer. I can't hold onto a job because she needs me to do everything for her, and she wanders off and gets into trouble, and I have to go and find her at all hours. I can't get a boyfriend, because as soon as they meet Junie, they stop calling.'

'Where did you go?' Connie asked, rubbing her arms: it was cold now, her clothes were still wet and her teeth were starting to chatter.

'Up to Penzance for a bit. I got an auntie up there. But I felt terrible, and I knew I couldn't leave Junie on her own, so I came back. Not in enough time, I s'pose.' Ellen looked down at the ground.

'So you were protecting Junie?'

'I've been protecting her all my life.' Ellen nodded, and started to cry.

Connie felt the anger leave her; she was too tired to be angry now, and too cold – but she was also realising that the real victim here was Ellen. It was clear that Junie should have had support from social services; but Fred had laid the responsibility for his wayward daughter at Ellen's door.

'I'm so sorry, Connie. You don't know how sorry I am. You were the first friend I had for years and years, and I messed it up. I meant it, you know. All that what I said at Biddy and Rosemary's graves. I wanted to put all this family rivalry behind us, but I failed. The Connors and the Christies. I thought we could change all that, but Junie ruined it.'

'Oh, goodness. Don't cry, Ellen.' Connie let go of Alex's hand and hugged the poor girl. 'This is such a mess, but it's over now.

Okay? I think we all just need to go home and go to bed, and deal with everything tomorrow. I'm exhausted and you must be too. All right?'

A strange calm had settled over Connie. She released Ellen from the hug, and nodded to her mum, who was sitting on the edge of the kerb back by the police car, drinking something from Adrian's flask and chatting away to him as if it was a pleasant morning on the beach and not past midnight after a dramatic chase.

'All right,' Ellen said, in a small voice.

'Alex, can you go and get Mum? She must be exhausted too...' Connie frowned. 'Although it does look like she's having quite a nice time talking to Adrian.'

'Sure.' Alex retreated, and retrieved Esther from her conversation. Connie noticed that Adrian looked quite disappointed, and touched Esther affectionately on the arm as they said goodbye.

'Will you be all right, Ellen?' Connie watched as Liza and Adrian closed the doors of the police car and drove away with Junie.

'Yeah. I've got to let Dad know what's happened, but no point calling round now. He'll have passed out,' Ellen sighed.

'Maybe now she's in the system, Junie might get the help she needs,' Connie suggested.

'Maybe. I dunno. I just can't protect her anymore, that's all.' Ellen wiped a tear away from her eye and flinched as she touched her own cheek, which was swelling up.

'I think you need to go and get that seen to,' Connie added, looking concerned. 'It looks nasty.'

'I'll go to the hospital tomorrow. Well, I doubt we'll be seeing much of each other from now on. So, goodbye. I'm sorry I couldn't be a better friend to you, Connie.'

'Goodbye, Ellen.' Connie watched the young woman walk off up the street and into the village. She did feel sorry for Ellen, but she was too tired to think about anything else now except her warm bed.

30

'So, what now?' Alex and Connie had left Magpie Cove's tiny police station, which was in fact a converted terraced house a few winding roads back from the high street.

Connie looked at the sky: it was going to be another beautiful day.

'Takeaway coffee on the beach?' Alex suggested, as they rounded the corner at the top of the high street. 'Maybe a late breakfast? I couldn't eat what your mum made earlier. I was too keyed up.'

It had been so late when they'd all got back to the Christie cottage that Alex had slept on the sofa. Yet, even though she'd got to bed in the early hours, Esther had been up at eight making a fried breakfast and chatting merrily to Alex as he rubbed sleep from his eyes and tried to keep up with her excitable stream of consciousness. By the time Connie had got up, had a shower and got dressed, Esther was already on the phone, relaying the night's events to one of her many friends that ran the Magpie Cove rumour mill. The story would be around the village by lunchtime, Connie thought.

'Sounds good. Extra shot for me, I think.' Connie rubbed her eyes. 'Don't you have to go up to the pub? Assess the damage?'

Alex groaned.

'Yes. But I feel like I need something in my stomach before I go up there. I'm dreading seeing it. Mind you...' He showed a series of texts on his phone screen to Connie. 'My dad and Tiny are up there already. Dad says it's not as bad as we thought. She's smashed a few windows and it looks like she tried to start a fire, but thankfully it didn't take. Other than that, it's just a big mess.' He breathed out a sigh of relief.

'I suppose there's only so much damage one smallish woman can do,' Connie reasoned.

'Come on now,' Alex retorted. 'Size has nothing to do with it.'

They'd just given their statements to Adrian in the station about the night before Junie Robb had also confessed that she'd been the one behind the cruel notes all those years ago, too, admitting that she'd "never liked that Connie" but also that "my memory's not that good. Sometimes I go in a dream, an' forget what I done".

'That's true,' Connie admitted.

'All right. I'll get us coffees and some bacon rolls. Wait here.' Alex nipped into Serafina's and Connie turned her face up to the sun, already high in the wide blue sky.

In her statement, Junie had said that she didn't like Connie and her 'fancy' ways, thinking she was so much better than everyone else just like all the Christies. And, that she knew Connie had broken Ellen's heart by seeing Alex, and so she'd sent Alex warnings too.

Junie had confirmed that Ellen had nothing to do with it. It was good to know that, Connie thought. She hadn't wanted to believe that it was all a pretence, Ellen being her friend. However, Adrian had told her that she had to make a decision: whether to press charges against Junie for the damage to the boat and the museum door or let the matter go. The notes didn't add up to much in themselves, although overall it could have been a harassment charge if Connie really wanted to go that far.

But did she? It was clear that Junie needed help more than anything. Liza, the policewoman, had suggested that Junie might be better off attending a local young women's support group that she led, alongside having a psychiatric assessment and any treatment deemed necessary. Connie had said she'd think about it, but as she stood outside Serafina's, she thought about how the café had changed in the past few years to operating on a pay-what-you-could basis.

Wouldn't it be better if something good came out of all of this, for her and for Junie? If she pressed charges, would that help anyone, really? Junie wasn't a hardened criminal. She was just a vulnerable girl who believed her father's lies, rooted in a genera-tions-old rift between two families. Like many in Magpie Cove, Junie needed help more than anything.

In fact, there wasn't really a decision to be made: there was little point in pressing charges, and the damage to the boat and the museum door was minimal anyway. She pressed the police station's number on her phone and spoke to Liza for a few moments, who agreed to register Junie for the support group.

Connie ended the call, knowing she'd made the right decision. Still with the phone in her hand, she looked at the email Georgia had sent about the stage manager job. Last night, she'd all but decided to leave, but now, things looked very different. Now that, hopefully, she didn't have to worry about someone messing with her livelihood, she had one less reason to go. But Georgia's offer had made her realise that she missed the theatre.

She was proud of what she'd done in the museum, but working in theatre was her true love. And she was good at it. She'd been good at the boat tours and welcoming people to the museum too, but there was something to be said about doing the thing you'd trained for, worked hard at, and were now well respected for. Connie's career had always been important to her. It was who she truly was: she loved it.

Connie looked away from her phone and through the big windows at the front of Serafina's, at Alex, who was walking back towards the door carrying two takeaway coffees and a brown paper bag.

Yesterday, trepidation had been pushing her to leave. Now, love wanted her to stay.

Connie and Alex were heading down the high street towards the beach when Connie heard someone shouting her name. She looked behind them and saw Hazel running towards them, waving.

'Hazel.' She smiled politely, not really knowing what to expect.

'Oh, Connie! I'm so glad I found you!' Hazel panted. 'Sorry. Shouldn't run in these heels.'

'Here I am.' Connie exchanged a glance with Alex.

'Oh, my goodness, you must think so badly of me!' Hazel cried, and, completely unexpectedly, threw her arms around Connie. 'Poor you, Connie! I just can't believe what's been going on!'

Connie disengaged herself as gently as she could from Hazel's embrace.

'Oh, right.' Connie was confused. She hadn't quite known what to expect after sending the message, but it had been a couple of weeks and she'd heard nothing from Hazel. In the meantime, everything else had happened.

'Your message. I'm so sorry I didn't reply, but we were in Spain on holiday and I couldn't get Messenger to work. Stupid phone.' Hazel frowned. 'But also, I thought I should come and see you in person. I mean, I appreciated the apology, but more than that, I just felt terrible for you. And I really, really wanted to assure you that it wasn't me leaving the notes and everything. I would never do that, you have to believe me,' Hazel finished slightly breathlessly. 'And then when I called your mum this morning, she told me everything. I can't believe it!'

'Oh,' Connie didn't know what to say. 'You were away in Spain?'

Hazel looked at her phone. 'Two weeks. We were in Valencia. Lovely villa there. All the pictures are on my Instagram. Look...'

She turned the screen to Connie, who noted the dates. Hazel had been in Spain when the *Pirate Queen* was vandalised and until yesterday.

'Ah. I see,' Connie let out a breath. 'So, that day when we had that argument...' she trailed off.

'I was annoyed, for sure. I let my mouth run away with me. I do that.' Hazel looked embarrassed. 'Dave tells me off about that all the time. I am trying to be better, but sometimes it still gets the better of me. Look, I can admit I judged those girls wrongly. I didn't really understand what they were trying to do. In fact, I've been looking at their Instagram and they're doing really well with the campaign. Did you know they've got over fifty thousand followers? And they've started a petition which has got loads of names. I've shared some of their memes.'

'That's awesome.' Connie nodded. 'I knew they were doing really well. We've talked about doing a follow-up film club. Maybe at *The Lookout*.'

'Well, I'll definitely be there.' Hazel smiled warmly. 'Look, I also wanted to say, I suppose I was annoyed at you because I'd tried to talk to you at Alex's pub opening, and you were a bit dismissive.' Hazel held up her hands in mock defence. 'It's okay, I understand why. I was kind of a bitch at school. I did actually want to say sorry for that.'

'Apology accepted.' Connie offered Hazel a wry smile. 'None of us are who we are when we were at school. Fortunately, I might add.'

'Well, what a drama, though!' Hazel laughed. 'I can't believe I missed it, actually. Makes me want to move back to Magpie Cove just so I don't miss out next time.'

'Be careful for what you ask for.' Connie giggled. 'Listen. We were just heading down to the beach, if you wanted to join us?'

Hazel looked from Connie to Alex, then at her watch.

'Ah, that's such a lovely offer, but I have to be off. I've got loads to do at home now we're back from holiday, but I just had to come and find you, Connie, and explain why I hadn't replied to your message. I just felt terrible. But... hey, can we maybe go for a drink? Maybe the four of us could go for a meal or something?' She looked hopefully at them both.

'Sure. That would be lovely.' Connie squeezed Alex's hand, who gave her a look that said, *See, I told you she wasn't all bad.*

'Great. Okay. Disaster averted.' Hazel mimed wiping her brow in mock relief. 'I'll call you, Connie. Your mum will give me your number.'

'I'm sure she will!' Connie replied as Hazel walked back up the high street. She exchanged glances with Alex.

Alex's eyes crinkled at the edges with suppressed amusement. 'Well, that was... interesting.'

'Oh, shut up.' Connie punched him lightly on the arm. 'I did really think it was her, you know. Leaving all the notes and stuff.'

'I know.' Alex rubbed his arm. 'Come on. Let's go.'

'So,' Alex began hesitantly, as they sat on the rocks at the back of the cove, watching the sun glimmer on the turquoise sea. He cleared his throat. 'I need to talk to you about something.'

'Okay...' Connie sipped her coffee and glanced at his face. He looked nervous. 'Is everything all right?'

'Yes. It's... I'm fine. I realised something last night. I've been stupid.'

'Well, I didn't want to be the one to tell you, but...' she joked, then saw the look on his face. 'Sorry. Not the time. Go on.'

'Okay. Well, you know I like you. You must know.' He met her eyes with his, gripping his coffee cup with both hands. 'But you were always pushing me away. Sometimes I got the sense that you liked me too, but then, like the other night after dinner, you just seemed so cold. And then I started to understand why. The stalking. You even thought it could have been me at first.' He took a deep breath. 'Don't get me wrong, I get it. But that was a hard thing to take on board.'

Connie nodded.

'Since Paula left me at the altar, I haven't had anything mean-
ingful with anyone else. I mean, I've had a few flings. I'm not a
monk. But there wasn't anyone I really let myself care for, because
I was afraid at failing again. That somehow it would all go wrong,'
he continued, holding the paper bag containing the bacon rolls on
his lap.

Connie rested her empty coffee cup on the sand and reached
for Alex's hand. He took hers, and squeezed it.

'I'm sorry,' she said, quietly. 'I was mean to you from the word
go, and I shouldn't have been. Also, can I have a bacon roll? I'm
starving.'

He smiled, and opened the bag, handing her a soft white roll
stuffed with perfectly crispy thick bacon and a generous dollop of
ketchup.

'Right. Remember the important things.' He took a large bite
out of his roll and paused for a moment. 'Anyway, what was I
saying? Oh, right. The thing is, when we were in that tunnel last
night, I was bloody terrified. I'm claustrophobic. I genuinely
thought I was going to die in there with you. But the only thing
that kept me from freaking out was knowing that I had to make
sure you were okay. And I imagined what it must have been like
for you and I just... I know it sounds naff, and you probably think
it's sexist and maybe it is, but I just felt like I wanted to be there to
protect you and make sure you never felt that way again. And I was
bloody furious at whoever had got me into that tunnel to chase
them.'

'Junie Robb.' Connie raised an eyebrow. 'I'm not sure she's
well, though. She said something about having times when she
doesn't remember what she's doing. To be honest, it sounds like she
has some mental health issues. At least now she can get the help
she needs.'

Alex shook his head. 'Sounds like Ellen's kept Junie out of
serious trouble for years now.'

'It's sad that a community can fail to notice when someone's struggling like that,' Connie added. 'Her and Ellen. They both should have had help a long time before now.'

'I know. Small communities like this, I think sometimes everyone just gets used to how people are and never think that they might actually need help. It's that old-fashioned way of just getting on with things. Changing slowly, but it takes time, I guess. Still, you'd have thought that the gossip mill should've realised something was seriously wrong,' Alex sighed. 'But, look. I don't want to get distracted here. I was saying something important.'

'All right, carry on then.' Connie twisted a tendril of her hair absently and tucked it onto her messy topknot.

'Fine. Now I've lost my train of thought...' He ran his hand through his hair. 'Oh, right. Well, I realised, in that tunnel with you, that I'd rather fail at love again with you than never try. So, this is me trying. I've fallen in love with you, Connie Christie. I want to be with you. For as long as you'll have me.'

Connie closed her eyes for a long moment.

'Alex, I... I really like you. And I want to be with you too. And I'm sorry I was so cruel to you, the other night... Don't let your bacon get cold, mind,' she added, taking another bite of hers.

'Okay.'

'You know I've been offered a job, back in Plymouth. Stage manager on a play, and then another one after that, probably. I'd have to leave Magpie Cove. The thing is, before all this happened, I'd pretty much decided I had to go. I thought, at the time... I thought it would be kinder to you if I just made a clean break with you before we got into a relationship.'

'Oh. I thought I'd done something wrong.' Alex's face relaxed; Connie could see relief in his eyes.

'No. I really wanted to go back with you, that night,' she looked away, blushing.

'You did?'

Connie gave him an exasperated look.

'Yes. You know I like you. And there's... you know... chemistry. Between us.'

His eyes twinkled. 'Chemistry, eh?'

'Oh, get over yourself. Eat your roll,' Connie laughed, despite the seriousness of the conversation. 'The thing is, now it's all over – the stalking thing – I don't *have* to leave anymore. But I still want to.'

Alex's face fell. 'Oh.'

'No, I don't mean it like that. I mean, I've loved the museum and the boat tours, but I'm a stage manager. That's what I do. It's what I'm good at, Alex. And as much as I want to see where things go with you, I also want that job. So, I want us to see each other. But I'm going to have to move. At least maybe between here and Plymouth. If I'm an hour or two away, that isn't such a big deal, is it? You can still drive over, or I can drive down?'

'Of course. We'll make it work. I was being an idiot the other night.' He enveloped her in a hug. 'I'd do anything for you.'

'You saved me from death in a disused smugglers' tunnel.' Connie hugged him back. 'I know you would. Listen to me, mister. Turns out you're my knight in shining armour after all, as mortified as I might be to admit it.' She grinned, looking up into Alex's deep brown eyes.

Alex gave her an amused look. 'I won't let you forget you just said that.'

'Cherish the moment. My mother will never believe I just said that either,' she replied.

'Oh, I will.' He drew her closer. 'So, what happens when the knight wins the femme fatale in those old movies you love?' he murmured.

'Well, femme fatales usually get killed off at the end of the film. For being too sexy for their own good. And knights win princesses and live happily ever after,' she corrected him. 'So, I don't know.'

He grinned. 'Oh, I see. Well, I think they say something incredibly cheesy, and then the camera pans away while they make out.'

'Oh, really? Like what?' Connie wrapped her arms around Alex's neck, and he lifted her up, high off her feet.

'Something like, *my heart called to you across the bridge of time*,' Alex replied, intentionally breathily, as she wrapped her legs around his waist.

'Wow. That's terrible,' Connie murmured, as their lips met. 'I think I prefer, *Now, kiss me, you fool*.'

31

FOUR MONTHS LATER

Connie didn't see Ellen at first. The museum was thronged with people laughing and talking, Christmas music was playing and the air smelled of mulled wine, oranges and fruit cake. She took a glass of champagne offered by a waitress and unbuttoned her coat. Outside, it was a crisp evening and she'd loved walking through the village and looking at all the Christmas lights strewn around the windows and doors of the little houses as Magpie Cove celebrated Christmas Eve.

Connie hadn't been back for a couple of months. She'd moved to a lovely little flat in Lostwithiel, an hour from Plymouth and about an hour and a half from Magpie Cove. The play had kept her pretty busy, with Alex staying a couple of nights a week. More recently, she'd been back to stay with him at the pub for a few days. She was happy, and in love.

Alex had said he was going to drop in, but Christmas Eve was a busy night at the pub. However, he'd called her earlier in the day to give her some good news: the strip of coast at Morven had succeeded in being added to Coastal Cornwall's preservation scheme, and work was going to start soon on shoring up the cliff-side. It was a huge relief; he'd tried not to show it, but Connie knew that Alex had been really worried he might have had to close the pub. Now, it looked as though they could stay open.

Her mum and Uncle Bill were already here, somewhere, but Connie couldn't see them yet. She ambled slowly around the museum, noticing what was different: some of the display cases were new and there was a children's activity centre in one corner that had never been there before. Connie knelt down, balancing her champagne glass on a blue bookshelf, and thumbed through the picture books, which were full of Cornish tales, fishermen and cats, and plenty about pirates. There was a rack of dressing-up clothes and a treasure chest filled with mermaid dolls and all manner of sea-themed plushies.

'Don't be shy – you can play with anything you want,' a voice said, shyly, behind her. 'Connie, I'm so happy you could make it.'

Connie looked up to find Ellen Robb standing next to her. She stood up, a stuffed octopus still in one hand.

'Hi, Ellen. Happy Christmas Eve!'

'Happy Christmas Eve to you, too.' Ellen did a nervous little dance. 'So, here we are.'

'The place looks wonderful! Thanks for throwing this lovely Christmas party, too. I'm sure Bill and Mum really appreciate it.' Connie put down the stuffed octopus a little self-consciously and picked up her glass of champagne instead.

'It's the least I could do. They've been so kind to me. You know, considering everything.' Sadness showed in Ellen's eyes for a moment before she banished it with a bright smile. 'And I owe it all to your kindness. I can't thank you enough, Connie. This job has changed my life.'

'It's my pleasure.' Connie was genuinely happy to see Ellen at the museum. There was a time when she wouldn't have believed it was possible, but Ellen Robb had turned out to be the perfect museum manager when Connie had left Magpie Cove.

At first, Esther and Bill had been dead against the idea. Esther, typically dramatic, had hissed, *Over my dead body!* And Uncle Bill had frowned and puffed on his pipe, until Esther remembered he wasn't supposed to smoke it and took it away.

Uncle Bill wasn't keen on the idea that the sister of Junie Robb, who had sabotaged his beloved *Pirate Queen*, would run the museum – *Not even countin', maid, that they're Fred Robb's daughters an' bad blood 'as flowed between these families for years*, he'd added.

But Connie had used all the skills she'd learned over the years in negotiating with bull-headed theatre directors to make them see what a good thing it could be to employ Ellen at the museum. And if Ellen was in charge, it set Connie free to go back to what she loved best.

'Look, Mum, Uncle Bill. I know it seems like Ellen would be the last person on earth you'd want to run the museum. But I believe that she had absolutely nothing to do with all the bad things that happened to me – in fact, when she found out what Junie was doing, she tried to stop her,' Connie had explained. She had told how Junie had been poisoned by her father's tales about the Christies from a young age and had believed it all – when in fact, he was a bitter man who resented Maggie marrying Bill and not him, and then took it out on the woman he married afterwards.

'No, maid. 'Tis not right. We can't have a Robb running the museum. The museum has always belonged to us, an' before it was a museum, 'twas the boat repair garage,' Uncle Bill had replied. 'Fred Robb allus wanted to get 'is 'ands on it, as well. I'm not 'andin 'im the keys now.'

Connie had argued that this had nothing to do with Fred – and, in fact, she'd talked to Ellen, and if she had a job, she could afford to move out of the flat that she'd lived in with Junie and find a place of her own. Nothing fancy, but the rents in Magpie Cove were lower than average. If Ellen worked at the museum, then she wouldn't have to be beholden to her father anymore.

They'd mulled it over, but what had decided it was Ellen herself. She'd come to the cottage a few nights before Connie was

due to leave, and brought an idea for the museum with her that
won Esther and Bill over.

'Come and see the new exhibit.' Ellen took Connie's elbow and
guided her excitedly to the other side of the room, where a crowd
surrounded something new.

Ellen had obviously worked very hard to achieve the new
display, which now adjoined Connie's Biddy Christie and the
Women of Cornwall area. Two mannequins, dressed in the fash-
ions of Biddy and Rosemary's time, were posed sitting at a table.
Ellen had gone to great lengths to get their hair right, based on old
photos of Biddy and Rosemary.

On the table, Ellen had arranged some of the old labelled
apothecary bottles her dad still owned, and laid out a notebook
belonging to Rosemary that detailed her study of herbal lore. Next
to Biddy, Ellen had carefully laid out some old folk herbals she and
Esther had found in the attic: books that detailed the medicinal
qualities of plants, sometimes with archaic and odd associations.
Behind them, Ellen had built a fake fireplace, on which she'd
placed Biddy's old cauldron, the one that Connie had found in the
attic months ago. One of Esther's old rugs sat under the table.

It looked for all the world as if Biddy and Rosemary had got
together one afternoon to brew up some herbal tonics or make
some salves, Connie thought. Somehow, she was immensely
touched. She read the detailed sign Ellen had written to accom-
pany the exhibit.

BIDDY CHRISTIE AND ROSEMARY CONNOR: A TRAGEDY OF MISUNDERSTANDING

Biddy Christie (1890–1941) and Rosemary Robb, nee Connor
(1887–1968), both lived at a time when women were slowly
gaining more independence, but had few of the freedoms we now
take for granted. Neither went to school, but Biddy's father taught
her to read and write, and Biddy took an interest in the natural
world around her, teaching herself about the plants and animals

around Magpie Cove from her own observations and from books like these. It looks as though she may have stolen these 'herbals' from a private collection, perhaps from a wealthy employer. Both books are inscribed M Cavanaugh, an unfamiliar name in the history of Magpie Cove – although there was a family named Cavanaugh living in Morven at that time. It may be that Biddy worked there for a time.

Rosemary's father, Abraham, taught Rosemary the apothecary trade that he had learned from his father, as she was the oldest of his three daughters. So it was that both young women shared a common interest.

Sadly, the Christie and the Connor families had a long-standing animosity between them, even before Biddy and Rosemary were born. It is believed that this dates back to the days when smuggling was rife on the Cornish coast, and the Christies and the Connors were embroiled in conflict over a lost shipment of brandy.

Rosemary's diary records that her grandmother told her that each side blamed the other for the loss of 500 bottles which, it had been agreed, were to be split equally between the families, them both having paid a well-known pirate up front for the goods. When the brandy never arrived, each family suspected the other of foul play.

Therefore, despite their common interest in plants and herbal medicine, Biddy and Rosemary were destined to be enemies from birth. Their respective diaries detail a number of arguments and misunderstandings over the years, the worst of which being the love triangle with Sam Robb, who would marry Rosemary and raise a family with her.

It is unclear what happened between them, but it seems that Biddy was in love with Sam, and was indeed having a relationship with him before he married Rosemary. After that, the animosity between the families only grew deeper.

It is easy to understand how historic grudges can prevail in small, largely insular communities such as Magpie Cove. Yet, it's a shame that Biddy and Rosemary were not allowed to be friends, because they had much in common and were both intelligent, witty and sometimes caustic women.

Therefore, we have created a place for them here, in the museum, where they can finally be friends. Who knows what good they might have both done if they had been allowed to pursue their studies, and their friendship?

'Ellen, that's... it's really wonderful. Thank you so much.' Connie felt quite emotional, reading what Ellen had written. 'And thank you so much for looking after the museum. Mum's told me what a great job you've been doing and I so appreciate it.'

'I'm just so glad you could come and see it.' Ellen beamed. 'I've been so worried about it! It's important to me that you think it's right. Is it right?' She scanned Connie's face nervously.

'Ellen, it's brilliant. I feel like you've managed to heal the rift between our families a bit, you know.' Connie stepped forward to get a better view. 'Acknowledging what came in the past, but that, I don't know, maybe we're moving past that now.'

'I hope so.' Ellen gave a shy smile. 'Your mum and uncle have been so sweet to me. They're even letting me stay at the cottage until I find a place to rent.' Connie laughed.

'Mum told me. She's not driving you mad yet, is she? Trying to marry you off, feeding you at all hours?'

'Oh, gosh, not at all. I love Esther. I wish I'd had a mum like that, growing up.' Ellen looked sad for a moment. Connie realised that, for Ellen, Esther's overbearing mumsy ways were actually the support she'd always needed and never had. 'And I don't mind her matchmaking me at all! In fact, I'm going out with someone next week. Clayton Bullock, from the boat shed. Esther invited him round for tea last week and we really hit it off. In fact, I was thinking I might ask Clayton if he wants to do the boat tours on the *Pirate Queen* next summer. Your uncle approves of the idea.'

'Wow! That's great, Ellen. I'm so happy for you.' Connie smiled at her friend. 'That sounds like a great idea. Clayton's a really nice guy and he knows boats. And how's Junie?'

'She's got a place at an assisted care place in Helston. I go and see her every week. She's actually much better now they've got her on some medication, too. And she loves that support group Liza runs.' Ellen reached out and touched Connie on the arm. 'I really can't thank you enough, Connie, for not pressing charges. In a funny kind of way, this whole thing has turned out to be good for Junie. And for me.'

'Oh, you don't need to thank me.' Connie wasn't sure what to say. 'But I'm glad Junie's doing so well.'

Esther made her way through the crowd around the exhibit, fanning herself.

'Now, then! My maid not even goin' ter say 'ello to her mother!' she cried.

Connie kissed Esther's cheek. 'Hi, Mum. Ellen was just telling me you've hooked her up with an eligible boat builder.'

'Not before time, an' all!' Esther crowed. 'An' where's your fella, missy? I've 'ardly seen my son-in-law recently, what with you leadin' 'im astray up Lostwithiel way.'

'He's coming in a bit, I think.' Connie looked around; Alex was pretty hard to miss. 'And please don't call him your son-in-law when he gets here. He's just my boyfriend. I don't want you pressuring him into anything.'

'I shall call him what I like, missy,' Esther replied, primly. 'An' it won't be long before there's a ring on yer finger, mark my words.'

Connie rolled her eyes at Ellen. 'Mum, have a day off.'

'What's she saying about me?' Alex's strong arms wrapped around Connie's shoulders in a hug and he nuzzled her neck. 'Hey, you.'

'Hey.' Connie turned around and kissed him; she felt that familiar melting she always did when she was anywhere near Alex.

It had been four months, and their chemistry hadn't fizzled out one bit. If anything, it had intensified. 'Happy Christmas Eve!'

'Happy Christmas Eve to you. It's frantic up at the pub. Though I see you guys have stolen quite a few of my regulars.' Alex surveyed the crowd with a smile.

'I was just sayin', Alex my love...' Esther stood on her tiptoes to plant a kiss on Alex's cheek. 'Won't be long now, will it? Before you propose to my Connie? Cos I'm not getting' any younger,' she added to Adrian, the policeman, who Connie only half-recognised out of his uniform.

'Aye, but you only get more beautiful,' Adrian replied, kissing Esther on the cheek. Connie did a double take.

'How long has this been going on?' she asked, incredulously.

'Oh, stop that face.' Esther flapped her hand at her daughter. 'A few months is all. I am allowed, ye know. Yer dad's been gone a long time now, God rest him.'

'I know! It's just... well, you didn't mention it,' Connie muttered. 'Anyway, ignore Mum's pestering about proposals. She's always sentimental around Christmas.'

Alex reached into his pocket and pulled out a small, black velvet box.

'Oh. You mean, I shouldn't do this?'

He knelt down in front of her, and Connie's heart skipped. This time it wasn't panic, or fear, though: this time, a wonderful warmth spread from her heart and made her whole body tingle.

The other partygoers standing near to them nudged each other and hushed; there were a few suppressed giggles.

'Oh God. Alex, what are you doing?' Connie whispered.

'Connie Christie, love of my life, most beautiful woman in Magpie Cove and the world, stage manager par excellence – oh, and one-time smuggling tunnel escapee – will you be my wife?' Alex asked, holding out a beautiful diamond ring.

Under Alex's smile, Connie knew there was an anxiety she'd say no: he'd been hurt before, and she never wanted to hurt his good heart.

But there was no danger of that.

'Yes,' she whispered, and Esther screamed in delight. The crowd cheered. Uncle Bill, from the counter, shouted out:

'Three cheers for the young lovers!' and the whole party shouted, 'Hip-hip-hooray!' as Alex grabbed Connie, lifted her up in his arms and kissed her deeply. When Connie opened her eyes, she caught sight of her mother's rapturous face as she watched them. Never mind being Connie's special moment: it was definitely all Esther had dreamed of for years.

'Oh, goodness. Can someone get my mother a chair before she falls over in shock?' she called out, still in Alex's arms. Everyone laughed.

'I love you, Connie Christie,' Alex murmured, his eyes drinking her in.

'And I love you, Alex Gordon,' Connie murmured back.

A LETTER FROM KENNEDY

Hello,

Thanks so much for reading *Daughters of Magpie Cove*. I hope you enjoyed it. If you did enjoy it, and want to keep up to date with all my latest releases, just sign up at the following link. Your email address will never be shared and you can unsubscribe at any time.

www.bookouture.com/kennedy-kerr

Cornwall's history fascinates me, and the perilous romance of its rocky coastline always makes me think of potential stories, especially in the days of the smugglers. Cornwall is a landscape made for drama with its tall cliffs and crashing waves, but it also contains little villages like Magpie Cove (which, to some degree, I based on the tiny coastal village of Cadgwith) which are cosy and small, but have hundreds of years of history in their bones.

In *Daughters of Magpie Cove*, I wanted to explore a story that reached back to the 1700 and 1800s and Cornwall's smuggling past, but also connected to the modern-day families in Magpie Cove: a family feud was, of course, an ideal solution. In Magpie Cove, generations of the Robb and Christie families have been at war, and I wanted two modern women to end it and be able to move on to new phases in their own lives.

I'm interested in the idea of ancestral trauma, and I do believe that we carry some of the trauma of the family that has come before us in our bones, or our minds and souls – however you want to think of it. Ellen, Junie and Connie manage to break the cycle of hatred between their families and start a new era in Magpie Cove, and I do believe that there's healing to be found for these old patterns. At the same time, we can see the younger members of the community standing up for their rights and refusing to be cowed by the ways things have been done before. They too are finding healing for themselves and the women of the future.

As ever, though, it wouldn't be a Magpie Cove book without lots of lovely food, a party or two and a few local Cornish characters to make sure there are a few laughs along the way – and, of course, a big hunk of a man with an even bigger heart.

Sending you lots of love and wishing you all the best that life has to offer.

Kennedy Kerr

facebook.com/kennedykerrauthor

twitter.com/@kennedykerr5

ACKNOWLEDGEMENTS

Readers interested in some of the UK's shipwreck and smuggling museums may like to visit or research the Shipwreck Museum at Hastings in East Sussex https://shipwreckmuseum.co.uk; the museum contained within the Jamaica Inn hotel in Cornwall (inspiration for Daphne Du Maurier's book of the same name) www.jamaicainn.co.uk/cornwall-museum and the Polperro Heritage Museum of Smuggling and Fishing in Cornwall http://heritagepress.polperro.org/museum.html, all of which provided inspiration for Bill's Shipwreck and Smuggling Museum in Magpie Cove.

You can find information about the famous Blackmore smuggling family and the Carter family from Prussia Cove online.

A note on the genealogy of the Christie family

For those interested in the generations between Biddy and Connie, I've dated their likely births as follow:

Connie is in her late twenties in 2021, so she could be born around 1993.

Esther was a youngish mum, married at nineteen and probably had her first baby at twenty-one. Connie is the third child, so

Esther was probably around twenty-five when she had her, which puts Esther's birth at 1968.

Esther's mother again would have had her at approximately twenty-five, so Connie's grandmother could be born in 1943.

Great-grandmother Mary could then be born in 1915, and great-great-grandmother Biddy could be born around 1890.

Printed in Great Britain
by Amazon